MUTANT BUNNY ISLAND

BY OBERT SKYE
ILLUSTRATED BY EDUARDO VIEIRA

HARPER
An Imprint of HarperCollinsPublishers

Library of Congress Control Number: 2017932866
ISBN 978-0-06-239912-0

Typography by Joe Merkel
17 18 19 20 21   CG/LSCH   10 9 8 7 6 5 4 3 2 1
❖
First Edition

To Henry V Santiago Wolfe.
My favorite Hank ever!
—O.S.

GETTING SQUIDDY WITH IT

The noise was loud enough to make me jump with fright. Something was tapping against my window, and that something didn't sound human.

"Newts!"

I slid my comic book under my pillow and quickly hopped off my bed.

There was no time to waste. I needed to act fast. Like Admiral Uli says, "Always wear pants, and always be prepared." Well, I was currently wearing pajama pants, but I wasn't prepared. For all I knew, a great newt storm was blowing my way right this second.

I took off my ocean-blue Admiral Uli reading glasses and slipped on a mask I'd made out of an old leather glove

1

and two rubber bands. Looking through the mask's fingers, I scanned my room. If only I had a proper ink blaster. Or my arms and legs were covered in suction cups. Not being a real squid, I was really at a disadvantage.

"Suction power!" I hollered, using my best Admiral Uli voice, which probably doesn't sound exactly like Admiral Uli. In fact, it kind of sounds like my neighbor with the high-pitched voice, who's always yelling at his cat.

The tapping grew louder, and I must admit, I screamed quite a bit.

The weather in Ohio isn't great to begin with, and now I was pretty sure the skies were dropping newt bombs. Thousands of newts were raining down on my house. Not normal newts, but the shifty, slimy, trench coat–wearing, devious, quasi-amphibian villains that are under the command of their nefarious leader, Figgy Newton. They drop from rain clouds or emerge from freshwater to cause trouble all over the world, especially for ocean dwellers like Admiral Uli.

I admit I was scared, but in the words of Admiral Uli, "When things look as dark as ink, always suck it up and get kraken."

Sure enough, just when I needed it most, I spotted a source of protection: my Admiral Uli Super-Sucking Tentacle Laser-Light Tube. I plugged it in and all the lights in the room flickered once. Then, with a loud snap, everything went completely dark. And in case you didn't know, completely dark is exactly how evil newts like it.

I might have screamed louder than before.

My dad came running down the hall. I guessed he wasn't very happy about having the power go out when he was using the bathroom. He also probably didn't like me screaming in the house. He pushed opened my bedroom door, and, even with no lights on, I thought I saw steam coming from his ears and off his bald head.

"Perry, are you okay?"

"I'm fine, but the world might be in peril," I said.

"The world's not in peril, buddy. Your toy tube blew a fuse again."

"You're not squidding. And we have bigger problems than that, because newts like it dark!"

My dad slapped his own forehead. He didn't always understand what I did or why I did it. "And you're wearing your mask again."

"Of course," I said. "These are dangerous times. A storm like you've never seen is blowing in."

"It's the beginning of summer, Perry, and the weather's nice."

My dad made his way to the window and threw open the curtains. The sun was rising in a blue sky dotted with small white clouds, and a tree branch lightly tapped against the glass. "See?" he said. "No peril. We're completely safe for the moment."

I love my dad, but he just didn't get me sometimes. I wished my uncle Zeke were here. He'd understand. Zeke is the greatest! He lives a long way from Ohio on a place called Bunny Island. He knows all about important things, like the United Squid Order and nefarious newts who are determined to destroy the oceans by removing all the salt. My uncle is also the one who sends me the copies of *Ocean Blasterzoids*. The series has been out of print for a long time, but Zeke has them all, and he mails me one every month without fail.

"I'm worried about you, Perry," my dad said. "You're cooped up in here all day. Kids need adventures. Sun, fresh air, scraped knees. You should go outside and play."

"No way! I'm not going outside," I informed him. "I don't trust nature. What if the newt-nado strikes?"

My dad didn't seem to want to hear anything about any kind of "nado." School had been out for one week, and I had already blown three fuses. He told me to sit in front of my window so that I'd get some sunshine. I was okay with that, seeing how newts hate the light.

My dad went to the basement to fix the breaker.

As I was staring out the window, my best friend, Ryan, pulled up to the house. I couldn't believe it! I had forgotten that he might show up today. I waved, but he didn't wave back. He probably couldn't see me. He got

4

out of a van and walked up our sidewalk. I ran from my room and opened the door just as Ryan rang the bell.

"Hello, Ryan!" I said.

Ryan pretended to sigh and then tried to hand me a wide orange envelope.

I should probably mention that Ryan is not only my best friend, he is also a driver for the UPP delivery company. He comes to my house once a month to deliver the latest comic from my uncle. I looked at the envelope and smiled at Ryan.

"Hello, Best Friend," I said, staring at him between the fingers of my mask.

"Look, kid, I'm not really your best friend. I'm the delivery guy."

"That's what you always say, but I know you're joking." He didn't laugh with me. "You're joking, right?"

"Please, just take the envelope," he said.

"Any sign of newts out there?" I asked. Sometimes changing the subject can be helpful when things are getting awkward. "Big ones, wearing trench coats?"

"I have no idea what you're talking about, kid. Please take the envelope."

"I'm just worried about your safety," I explained. "I can't have my friends in danger."

"Once again, we're not friends. Here."

Ryan dropped the orange envelope and turned to walk

away. It wasn't unusual for Ryan to be moody, so I forgave him. But not for the first time, I wondered whether it might be nice to have friends who were actually friendly.

I ran to my room and fell on my bed. Down in the basement, I could hear my dad struggling to get the lights back on and using words that I probably shouldn't repeat. Luckily, the open curtains in my room let in enough light for me to see.

I carefully pried up the edge of the envelope. Slowly, like I was pulling a hot personal pizza from the oven, I pulled out the comic book. I couldn't believe my eyes. Instead of it being the next issue, it was a special edition of *Ocean Blasterzoids*.

"*Salt Wars.*" I was breathless.

There had only been a few of these printed. I knew my uncle had one, but he had never let me see it. Now here it was in my own hands. The story of how Uli grew up and was betrayed in the early salt wars.

My uncle had shown great trust in me by sending this. Uncle Zeke always treated me more like an adult squid than a little kid.

The cover of the special edition showed Admiral Uli standing at attention. His two steel-tipped tentacles were coiled up into metal fists. In his third arm he was gripping his ink blaster, and in his fourth, a small net. I triumphantly held the comic book above my head.

At that exact second, the lights in our house came back on.

It was like a comic book miracle. As I was lowering the issue, a small piece of paper slipped from the pages and drifted to the ground.

"Great inky beak," I whispered, using one of Admiral Uli's many useful catchphrases.

I picked up the little white piece of paper. On one side it was blank, but as I flipped it over, I gasped. There, scratched on the back in jagged letters, was one single word. It was written in another language, but I'll translate:

HELP

I gulped. This was bad. Uncle Zeke was in trouble.

CHAPTER TWO

SNACK PACK

I didn't know what to do. It's not like I could just show the note to my dad. First off, he wouldn't understand it, seeing how it's written in Admiral Uli's home language, Cephalopodian. That's a long word I know, but it's what everyone speaks in Cephalopodia, one of the great nations beneath the sea. It's also the language that my uncle Zeke and I learned so that we could be more like our hero.

Oh, I just remembered a joke my uncle told me the last time we talked on the phone. He said, "Ooit diven doo sqawtle pip."

And I had answered, "Wip ta."

It was hilarious. Trust me, you'd be laughing so hard right now if you spoke Cephalopodian.

Of course, most of the kids at my school don't know or appreciate *Ocean Blasterzoids*, and they certainly don't care where Admiral Uli lives. In fact, Matt Blip, a fellow fifth grader who has tiny teeth and big ears, once told me how he thought *Ocean Blasterzoids* was for nerds. Then he gave me a circus wedgie—which is like a regular wedgie except after they pull up your underwear they swing you by it like you're on a trapeze, while making circus-music noises.

I don't care for Matt Blip.

I do like my uncle Zeke though. He believes in the newt threat, and we promised each other that if either of us were ever in trouble we would let the other one know. Now he had sent me a cry for help!

I flipped through the comic book again to see if there were any other clues. There were! Chewed into the last page were three letters even more frightening than the note:

MEL

Yeah, I was pretty shocked, too.

Every wannabe squid worth his weight knows that the Cephalopodian word for *newt* is "mel."

It was now perfectly clear what had happened: my uncle had been overtaken by newts, and I was his only hope. I was scared for him, but happy that he believed in me enough to send the signal. I also knew there wasn't much time. Newts were notorious for taking prisoners and then getting rid of them when they grew bored. And because of their small brains, newts grew bored quickly.

I wanted to tell my dad what was happening, but after he got the lights working again he went back into the bathroom. Plus, even though his brother, Uncle Zeke, was a believer, my dad wasn't. He didn't like comic books. He liked boring things like working as a fact checker for an insurance company and gardening. I think he secretly wished he was a farmer. His favorite magazine (the one he was probably reading in the bathroom right now) is called *Let's Talk Wheat*. Who in their right mind wants to talk wheat?

He also loves *The Old Farmer's Almanac*, which is a book that tells you everything you need to know about farming. But he doesn't just use it for farm advice, he uses it to help him be a better dad. Last week he brought me a glass of water while I was watching TV because he was reading about the dangers of inconsistent watering. He's always looking out for me, but he really has a hard time knowing what to do sometimes. That's why there was no way I could drag him into this. Besides, something in my shaking body knew that this was a task I needed to do by myself. Sure, I'm just a kid, but I know more about newts and their evil ways than almost anyone. I would have much more luck saving my uncle if I was on the case without my dad. Of course, I couldn't help from here in Ohio, which meant I was going to have to leave the comfort of my home and my computer and my room and my TV and travel to Bunny Island.

I shivered just thinking about it.

"What would Admiral Uli do?" I whispered, trying to sound brave.

I could almost hear the admiral whisper back, "When the danger is great, swim with speed, and don't pee in the ocean."

I could be brave. Uncle Zeke needed me, and there was no way I was going to let him down. It was important that I swam or moved as quickly as possible. I ran to the bathroom and pounded on the door.

"Occupied!" my dad yelled.

"It's an emergency," I yelled back.

I heard him using a few salty words, followed by the sound of the toilet flushing. The door opened and he stared down at me while holding a copy of *Amazing Grains* magazine under his right arm.

"You're still wearing your mask," he said.

"Thanks for noticing," I replied. "But no time for compliments. Uncle Zeke wants me to come visit him."

"He does?" my dad asked. "That's nice, but does he

know you barely leave your room?"

"Yes, but I told him I would."

"You did?" My dad coughed for a few moments before he added, "But Bunny Island is . . . well, it's supposed to be kind of an odd place."

"Odd how?" I asked.

"I've never been, but Zeke says it's filled with bunnies and health food and grass and nature. What about your allergies?"

"I think there are worse problems in this world than allergies, Dad. I'll be okay."

"But, Perry, I don't understand. You hate fresh air and sunshine."

"I've changed."

Everything I was saying was untrue. I don't like nature, and I don't like lying to my dad, but Uncle Zeke was in trouble.

"It does sound like fun, kiddo," he said seriously. "But I'm afraid I can't get the time off work."

"I could go by myself," I suggested.

"What? You'd go by yourself?"

I nodded. Yes, I was a little terrified by the thought of leaving my house and going it alone. There would be newts out there for sure, and sometimes newts try to pass as regular people, which can be confusing, not to mention terrifying. Still, I knew flying to Bunny Island alone was what I needed to do.

"This sounds like an amazing adventure for you, Perry. How long would you be gone?"

"I'm not sure," I said. "Maybe two weeks?"

My dad was always talking about how important adventure was to a young boy. He picked up the almanac and flipped through it, looking for advice that might have to do with his son going off to a faraway island by himself. "You know, I've been reading about the benefits of crop rotation. Young shoots do need a wide variety of nutrients, and you're a young shoot," he said. "Maybe it would be wise for you to spend some time on different soil. And who knows, I suppose you could be a real pick-me-up to your uncle."

"I'm too big to pick up."

My dad ignored my comment. "Of course, I don't know what I'd do without you. When did your uncle say you should come?"

"As soon as possible."

"I'd miss you, but it would be the trip of a lifetime. Would you actually spend time outdoors? Do you think you'd run on the beach and climb trees?"

"Who knows what the future will bring? But I've never seen the actual sea before. I've always been stuck here with newt-filled freshwater lakes and rivers."

"Well, then this needs to happen."

My dad dropped his almanac and ran to his computer. I remained standing where I was, wondering if I was doing the right thing. I knew my uncle needed me. I just hoped I was brave enough to go through with this.

Not finding what he needed on the computer, my dad called the airport. I could hear him asking some questions. Then he put his hand over the bottom part of the phone and turned to me. "The only flight going to Bunny Island this week leaves in less than two hours, and there's just one seat left!"

"Two hours?" I asked as I walked over to him.

"You should wait a week," my father suggested. "We can prepare and—"

"I can't wait that long," I interrupted. "I think Uncle Zeke needs . . . wants me to come as soon as possible."

"Really? Well, the airport is practically next door," my dad reminded me. "And if you make the flight, you'd be on Bunny Island by late afternoon."

"Then we should move," I said excitedly.

My dad looked like he was about to reach for the almanac to seek advice, but instead he put his hand on my shoulder and smiled.

"Perry," he said seriously. "Those trees on Bunny Island aren't going to climb themselves. Let's get you to the airport."

I don't normally like being rushed into things, but my

uncle was in trouble, and there wasn't a second to waste. I looked at my dad and nodded like a brave and noble squid.

My dad removed his hand from the mouthpiece of the receiver and told the airport person that we wanted the ticket. He gave some additional information and then hung up. "Shake the wheat out, Perry, we need to hurry!"

"I'll go pack," I said.

"That should be easy." He jumped up. "Just throw all the clothes from your dresser into a couple of suitcases. I'll help."

"That's okay," I said, thinking of a few extra items I'd need. "You go start the car. I'll take care of it."

"Okay, big guy," my dad said with a whistle. "I'll start the car."

Suddenly, I felt too nervous to do this. But I kept my mouth shut and ran down to the basement to get two big suitcases. After hauling them back upstairs I wheeled them to the kitchen. Sure, I was supposed to pack things like clothes and toothbrushes, but if I was going to some strange nature island, I needed snacks. Like I really needed them. They were the one thing that I couldn't live without.

I threw open the cupboards and started cramming snack food and treats into the two suitcases. Luckily, we had just stocked up for summer, so we had tons of good things. I filled one suitcase with all the sugary treats I could fit. I crammed the second one with my favorite thing in the world—potato chips. We had about ten different kinds.

My dad gave a quick tap on the car horn in the garage.

"Coming!" I yelled.

I could barely get my suitcases closed. I took off my mask and put it into one of my pant pockets.

My dad honked some more. I needed to move.

I grabbed the last bag of chips left in the cupboard and shoved it under my arm. They were my favorite flavor—Munchables—sugar dipped and extra-salty.

"Coming!" I yelled again.

I ran to my room and grabbed the orange envelope that held the collector's issue of *Ocean Blasterzoids* and my uncle's note. It also had his address on the front. I slipped the envelope into the pocket of my suitcase. With the extra potato chips under my arm, I dragged my luggage into the garage. My dad hopped out of the car and took the suitcases from me. He threw them into the trunk and jumped back in.

"All set?" he said. "Lucky for you, the airport's just a couple miles away!"

My dad really didn't need to tell me that. We could hear the planes flying over our house all the time.

He backed out of the garage and we raced down the

street. I couldn't see any newts raining down, but to be perfectly honest, I was now more afraid of what lay ahead of me.

"I think we might make it!" my dad said. "I'll call your uncle and tell him when to pick you up."

"That's okay," I said quickly. "I talked to him on the phone just now. That's why it took me so long. He said he'll pick me up."

"Way to be responsible," said my dad, which kind of stung since everything I was saying was a lie.

My dad sped down the highway at an irresponsible speed. I double-checked my seatbelt and tried to calm my nerves.

We turned off the highway onto the airport road. It was all happening so fast. I had questions. A lot of questions. I tried to ask the most important ones.

"Flying on a plane is safe, right?"

"The only thing safer is riding on an elevator," he answered.

"I don't like elevators," I reminded him.

"Well, good thing you're taking a plane."

Inside the airport, a man at the ticket counter took my luggage, but I held on to my extra bag of chips. My dad and I jogged toward the security line.

"You'll need some cash when you get there," Dad said. He reached into his wallet and emptied it out.

"Thanks," I said, taking the wad of cash from him.

"Have a blast, kid," he said. "Call me as soon as you get to Zeke's, and remember I'll be thinking of you every second."

"That's a lot of seconds."

"I'm so glad you'll be doing something other than staring at your computer or reading in your dark room. This is it, Perry, your summer begins now!"

"Thanks, Dad."

His goofy grin made me realize I was going to miss him and Ohio worse than a severed tentacle. I had never been out of the state and I had never been away from my father. I kept telling myself over and over in my head that all of this was for Zeke.

"Have fun, and call me every day," my dad said.

"I wish we could communicate like squids. Their skin lights up in ways that only other squids can understand."

"Well, until we have that ability, use the phone."

"I'll miss you."

"And I'll miss you back. Now, I'm double-parked so I have to go. Plus, I'm just not good at good-byes."

"Bye, Dad."

"Let's just say, 'Grains be with you until we wheat again.'"

"That's awful," I said, smiling.

My dad hugged me and helped me up to the front of

the line where he turned me over to the airport employees. Since I was a kid traveling alone, a security lady showed me what to do. I emptied the many pockets on my cargo pants as quickly as I could. I had way more stuff in my pockets than I remembered.

The lady set my carry-on potato chips on a conveyer belt and walked me to the full-body scanner, where I had to hold my hands up in the air like a criminal newt getting apprehended by the squid patrol. My Admiral Uli belt buckle made the machine beep loudly, so I had to take it off. While I was walking into the machine for the second time, my pants fell to the ground.

"Hold perfectly still," the lady said. "Still scanning."

I stood there like a statue in my Admiral Uli skivvies while people in the line behind me tried not to laugh and failed. I looked to see if my dad was laughing, too, but he was on the other side of security waving at me as if everything was perfectly normal.

I pulled my pants up, and a different security woman with big hands helped me away from security and down to my gate.

I was going to Bunny Island to confront the newts and save my uncle. And I had no idea how weird and scary Bunny Island would be.

CHAPTER THREE
BUNNY ISLAND

Squidships are probably great, but it turns out planes are a pain. After the first long ride, I had to stop at another airport and switch to a different plane before that one finally landed on Bunny Island. The second plane was really small and filled with old people who kept talking and singing. I did get to look at my new "Salt Wars" comic book, but that was the only highlight.

When the plane touched down, the flight lady turned on the speaker and said, "Welcome to Bunny Island—where the temperature is just right and the fruit is so fresh you can flirt with it."

Gross.

Everyone on the plane laughed and clapped except

for me. I was already scared about there not being enough junk food. Now I was supposed to flirt with fruit? If it had been anyone else in trouble besides my uncle Zeke, I would have stayed in my seat and refused to exit.

Stairs led straight from the plane to the tidy runway. As soon as I stepped outside, sunshine blasted my eyes. Instantly, I began to sweat and worried that I might wither like a jellyfish on a hot sidewalk.

At the bottom of the stairs stood a woman with flowers in her hair. She was handing out round fluffy tails for people to stick on their behinds. She dropped one in my hand and said, "Welcome to Bunny Island."

"Do I have to put this on?" I asked, knowing Admiral Uli would never wear something as embarrassing as a bunny tail. "I'm more squid than land animal."

"It's our custom," she said.

She looked so hurt that I took the small tail and stuck it to my behind.

Inside the airport, large banners hung from the ceilings and fluttered in the air-conditioning. On each banner was a smiling man with slicked-back hair and shiny blue eyes. One of the banners showed him saying:

Welcome to Bunny Island—
America's 37th Favorite Vacation Spot!

Another one had him drinking a green smoothie and saying:

Bunny Island: 100% Junk Food–Free

My sugar-covered heart almost had a heart attack! I knew that Bunny Island was supposed to be filled with health nuts, but I didn't know it was junk food–free. And that wasn't even true anymore, because at that very moment, my snack-filled suitcases came sliding down a silver chute onto the baggage carousel. Now there were at least two suitcases full of junk food on the island.

I felt like Admiral Uli in Issue #32, when he smuggled crab kittens away from the wetlands of Mewmar.

I wrestled my first suitcase off the luggage carousel. As I was struggling to get a hold of the second one, someone's hand shot out and grabbed it for me.

"I got it."

I turned to find a boy who was probably a few years older than me. He had long wavy bangs that hung over his big brown eyes. His teeth were straight and white and his shoulders were way wider than mine. He was wearing a tank top with the words Rain Train on it and shorts that came to his knees. Also, he was dark-skinned and cool looking. I suddenly felt extra pale and dorky.

"Your suitcase smells," the boy said. "Like food."

"It's not food, it's just some old shoes." I wasn't proud of it, but I was getting good at lying.

"It's got a strange vibe."

"That's probably the lingering foot odor."

"Okay, no worries. Let me carry your bags."

"Who are you?" I asked.

"I'm Rain."

"Wow, that's a cool name, except for the fact that newts can travel by rain cloud."

He stared at me.

"I'm Perry, by the way, and just to be completely honest and forthright, I'm ten."

There was nothing but silence for a moment.

"So," he finally said. "I guess ten-year-olds have tails."

I forgot I was wearing the puffy white bunny tail. Now here I was meeting what might be a new island friend, and I looked like a baby bunny. I reached around, pulled it off my behind, and threw it over my shoulder like it had the kind of cooties that other cooties made fun of.

"So do you need a ride somewhere?" Rain asked.

An invitation for a ride? That was definitely something a friend would ask.

"You can drive?" I said. "How old are you?"

"I'm thirteen, and I can sort of drive. I have my own business—the Rain Train. I take people around the island

and point out interesting things."

"In a train?"

"Of course not. It was the only mode of transportation that rhymed with my name."

"So you have a car?"

"It's like a car."

"Well, I do need a ride," I said. I unzipped the front pocket of one of my suitcases, pulled out the envelope with my uncle's address on it, and showed it to him. "Do you know where that is?" I asked.

Rain smiled. "I know exactly where that is. It's a straight shot down Rabbit Road through town and past the mall and the beach. It's in the Gray Hare subdivision. I can take you, but it'll cost you some money."

"That's fine. I've got a wad of cash."

Rain's eyes grew stormy. "You know, I really can't stand you Bunny Mooners sometimes."

"Bunny Mooners?"

"Yeah, that's what we locals call you tourists," Rain said. "You come to our island and brag about your wads of cash. That's not very cool."

"I wasn't bragging. I just don't have a wallet."

"Whatever, I need the money. Come on." Rain motioned for me to follow him.

I wasn't sure I wanted to go. To be honest, Rain was seeming a little newt-like, but I had no other ride, and the clock was ticking. My uncle wasn't going to save himself. I needed to get to his house and start looking for clues.

I followed Rain outside. A straight road ran from the curb down toward the beach in the distance. I had seen the ocean in pictures and movies, but here, it was a completely different thing—enormous and turquoise blue, like the color of Admiral Uli's friend Stacy Horse. I could smell the salt from where we stood. Looking at the water, it was easy to imagine a whole world of squids and death-defying adventures hidden beneath the surface. I shivered with excitement and uneasiness.

"I've never seen the ocean before," I whispered.

"Well," Rain said. "There it is."

The island was covered with palm trees that looked like giant green scrub brushes. Along the road, tall wooden poles supporting large megaphones poked up at regular intervals. I knew from what my uncle had told me that the megaphones were a warning system, in case there was ever a tidal wave coming. At the moment, the sky above us was completely clear, and a hot wind swirled around me like an annoying ghost.

"Is it supposed to be this warm?" I asked. "I have sweat in places I've never sweated before."

"That's lovely."

I spotted a motel with a large rabbit-shaped statue on the roof and a park where a couple of families were flying kites. A few people puttered down the road in golf carts, followed by a large woman on a Segway and a girl on a skateboard. The scene looked like the front of a fancy but sort of weird postcard—a postcard for a place that everyone but me would want to visit.

I was hot and uneasy, and I missed my room.

To make things even stranger, everywhere I looked, I started to notice real, live bunnies quietly hopping around and resting in every available spot of shade. I didn't have any pets back in Ohio because I preferred animals to be in books or on the computer screen—there are way less allergies that way. Now, however, it looked like I was surrounded by a billion bunnies.

"So many rabbits," I said, punctuating my statement with a sneeze.

"Yep," Rain agreed. "You Bunny Mooners can't stop taking pictures of them and trying to pick them up."

"I'm not a Bunny Mooner, and I don't even have a camera," I said, kind of wishing I did. "Where'd all the rabbits come from, anyway?"

"That's a long story that I don't have time to tell. Now hop on."

Rain motioned to an old green bike parked at the curb. It had an extra back seat and a cart hooked to the rear. A small horn was clipped on the handlebars.

"That's what we're riding?" I asked. "That's not a car

or train or even a normal bike."

It reminded me of one of the worthless machines that Eelbert Brinestein was always tinkering with.

"Look around," said Rain. There are no real trains or cars on the island—just golf carts and Segways and bikes."

He put my suitcases on the cart behind his bike and tied them down tightly with yellow bungee cords. I climbed on the backseat and put my hands on Rain's shoulders. The adhesive left over from the bunny tail sort of helped hold me in place.

"Welcome to Bunny Island," Rain said. "For the next few minutes I'll be your tour guide."

"I don't really need a tour," I told him. "But I do need to get to my uncle's place. Maybe I should just borrow your bike and pedal myself? I've got pretty strong ankles."

That was probably the wrong thing to say, because Rain's neck got red and he started to huff.

"You think all my business needs is strong ankles? You wanna take over my gig? I know a heck of a lot more about this island than you do."

"I don't want to take over your business," I insisted. "I just need to get to my uncle's. Fast."

"Fine."

Rain took a few deep breaths and calmed down. He shook his butt as though swishing an invisible tail from side to side before settling down on the bicycle seat. For a second his movement reminded me of a newt, and it gave me the chills. He pressed the horn on the handlebars.

BUUUUURRRRRRRUUUUUUUPPPPA!

A powerful toot sounded and the packs of bunnies directly in front of us scattered. I held my hands over my ears as Rain tooted the bike horn once more. It wasn't a newt toot, but still, something smelled off.

"Ready?" Rain yelled.

I nodded.

"Oh," Rain added. "I forgot to tell you that my bike has no brakes."

"What?"

"You heard me."

"But—"

Rain took off before I could finish my sentence, leaving my "but" hanging in the air.

CHAPTER FOUR

BIKE RIDE OF DOOM

The Rain Train flew down the path. We were moving so fast, I couldn't hear my own screams. As we hurtled along, my life flashed in front of my eyes. I saw all the times I had been at home alone in my room eating toast dipped in chocolate spread and sprinkled with taffy. I saw myself lying in bed and reading comics and eating butter-covered chips. I also saw the time I was sick from eating too much.

I really missed home.

"Can you please slow down?!" I yelled. "I have a fear of dying."

"Sorry, no brakes. I'll try going faster." Rain started to pedal harder.

"But I'm pretty sure that's the opposite of slowing down!"

I looked around for seat belts or an ejector seat, like Admiral Uli had in his squid sub, but there wasn't anything like that. We bounced down the stone road like a couple of rubber balls. All around us, bunnies of all colors were hopping and jumping out of the way. One orange bunny hit my right leg and then sprang off me. A gray one shot out from the trees and hopped as high as my head.

Rain blew the horn, lifted his butt off the seat, and leaned into the turns. He swerved around a tall palm tree and shot past a fuzzy herd of bunnies parked by the side of the path.

"I-I-I-I-I can't p-p-p-p-p-p-p-pay you if I'm d-d-d-d-d-d-dead!" I yelled as we bumped along.

"Don't worry," he yelled back. "I can always take the money from your wad of cash! Look, there's the Bunny Hotel! That's where most of the Bunny Mooners stay when they come here." Rain lifted his right hand off the handlebars to point at the motel with the bunny statue on the roof as we blew by.

"Hold on to the handlebars!" I begged.

Rain let go with both hands and did some more pointing. "Down the road to the left is the Liquid Love Shack. That's my mom's business—she makes the best carrot juice in town."

"Yuck!" I shouted.

Sure, I was scared for my life, but I wasn't scared enough to say something nice about carrot juice.

"It's not really for Bunny Mooners," Rain yelled. "It's a local hangout. There's the golf course and the health food store. And the . . ."

Rain was pointing like a crazy man. I wanted him to put his hands back on the handlebars and find a way to slow down. I could see a large herd of bunnies up ahead. I could also see a group of people blocking the path, holding up their phones to take pictures of bunnies.

Rain lay on the horn and yelled, "Coming through!"

The people just stood there as Rain swerved around them.

"Bunny Mooners!" he yelled. "No matter what happens, they never notice anyone but themselves! They come here and think they're all that matter. They should really work on their self-awareness."

I sort of thought Rain could do a little work on his own.

"Oh, there's the mall. It's one of the few places with air-conditioning."

The mall didn't look that different than most of the malls I had seen in Ohio. The only difference was that on the top, there was a giant pair of bunny ears sticking up.

"Could you pleeeeeease try and stop!" I pleaded.

"I can't," Rain said happily. "There really are no brakes! We'll need something to crash into when we want to stop. But don't worry, the universe always provides a way."

"I don't think we should be friends!" I yelled.

"I'm thirteen! I wouldn't be friends with a ten-year-old for anything. Especially a Bunny Mooner!"

"Okay, fine! Why doesn't your bike have brakes?!"

"I built it myself. I'm still saving up for them!"

We whizzed past a field filled with flowers that looked like pink suction cups. Rain swerved to miss a brown bunny and hit a tree root that was stretched out across the sidewalk. The bike bounced two feet up and came down, hard.

I looked back to make sure my suitcases were still okay. One of the yellow bungee cords was slipping off! This was now a life-or-starve situation—my snacks were in danger. And who would save my uncle if I died of starvation? Rain bounced over another root. If only I had been born with tentacles, I could wrap them around Rain, grab the handlebars, and bring this dangerous ride to a stop.

I raised my fist to the sky and cursed the universe for only giving me two puny arms.

As the bike shook again, I did the only thing I could: I imagined my arms and legs were tentacles and wrapped them as far as I could around Rain's body. I hung on to him like a limited edition Admiral Uli backpack.

I'll be honest—it wasn't my finest idea.

Rain hollered as I bound both his arms and caused him to take his hands off the handlebars again. The bike raced down the road. It shot out from between two palm trees and rocketed onto a bumpy dirt path.

"Let go of me!" Rain yelled.

"For the love of lobsters, stop this bike!"

"I can't steer while you're holding me."

The bike raced down the path with both of us still on it. Ahead I could see white sand covering everything like a heavenly coating of sugar and salt. Beyond that, ocean. Between the dirt road and the beach was a curb made of rocks.

"Let go!" Rain screamed again.

I let go and unwrapped my legs so Rain could grab the handlebars and pull up. The front wheel popped over the rocky curb and we went whizzing between two golf carts and onto the sandy beach.

Ahead of us were three grown men working on a large sand castle. A normal person would have tried to avoid them, but Rain wasn't normal. He steered directly toward their creation. The three men waved and yelled, but nothing they shouted helped slow us down, and we plowed into the sand castle with a giant

WHACKTHUDSMOOSH!

Rain and I flew off the bike and into the ocean. Waves splashed all around me as I frantically tried to pull myself above the water. I thought I was going to drown until I remembered I was actually a pretty good swimmer. I had begged my dad for lessons when I was seven, right after I nearly drowned in a large puddle of rainwater because I was pretending it was a portal to a different world. Anywho, now those swimming lessons were really paying off.

I swam toward the shore fighting the waves and marveling over how salty the water tasted. It reminded me of Admiral Uli and of the mashed potatoes my dad made. He always oversalted everything, which was just the way I liked it.

I really missed him.

At the edge of the water I sat down and coughed and choked while pulling bits of seaweed out of my hair. I felt like I was under attack from a wet salad. And I was soaked in both body and mind. I had always wanted to see the ocean, but I had hoped for a better introduction. A few feet to the right of me, Rain stepped out of the waves.

The three men were staring at what used to be their large castle. Now it was just a sand dump with a bike sticking out of it. My suitcases had broken the bonds of bungee and were lying near the water on dry land.

Rain walked up to me and stuck out his hand to pull me up.

"You're pretty tough," he said. "I probably should have told you about the brakes before you got on."

I guessed that was his version of an apology. "That would have been nice," I said.

Rain opened his palm and held it toward me. Not knowing what to do I slapped it and gave him five.

"Actually, you owe me ten dollars."

"Oh, is there any discount for almost dying?"

"Nine dollars is fine."

"Also, we're not even at my uncle's house."

"I'll take eight then. And his house is two blocks that way." Rain pointed to a street at the end of the beach. "It's just past that glass payphone."

As I stood up, water drained from all the pockets of my green cargo pants. I fished out some wet money and handed it over.

"If I can ever be of service again, just let me know," Rain said.

I was too frustrated and wet to even reply.

He pulled his bike out of the sand while the sand castle builders yelled. I collected my suitcases and did a quick inspection. They were both sandy but otherwise okay. If they had landed in the water, my life and appetite would have been ruined for good.

I pushed the buttons on the handles and pulled them up.

I dragged my suitcases through the sand and toward the Gray Hare subdivision. My sneakers sloshed with water and made disgusting noises with every step I took.

So far Bunny Island was sweaty and wet. I missed my dad, Rain had almost killed me, and my butt was itchy from sand. On the brighter side, I had finally swum in the ocean, which was something all wannabe squids should do. I thought about stopping for a moment to give myself a high five, but I didn't. Not only was my uncle in trouble, but it sounded like someone was following me.

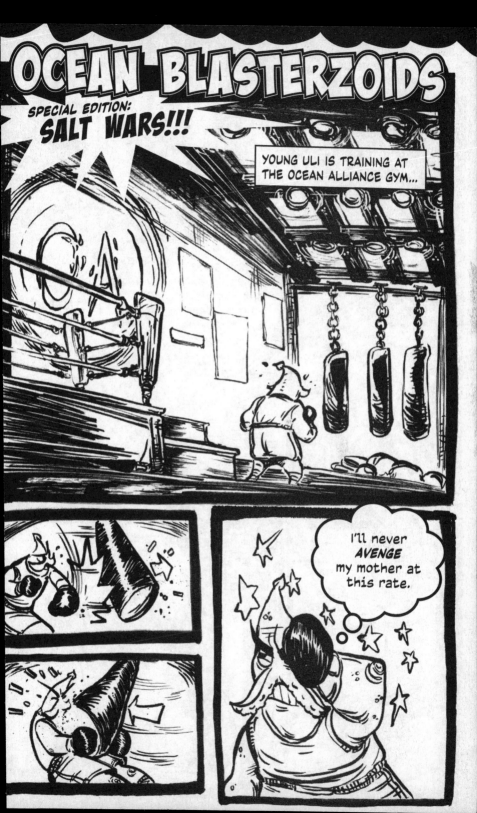

CHAPTER FIVE
JUST LIKE I THUNK, NO UNK

As I continued up the street toward my uncle's house, I was sure I heard something coming up behind me, clicking and scraping like a newt with a bionic metal tail. My heart began to pound, and sweat dripped on my forehead. I looked straight ahead and tried to stay calm. I wasn't in the mood to fight anything. Actually, I would probably never be in the mood. Sadly, I had no real fighting skills. I had always wanted to learn karate or kickboxing or cephalopod slap dancing, but the only thing I knew how to do was kick blindly and run.

I picked up my pace, still dragging my suitcases and listening carefully to whatever it was behind me. It didn't really sound like the footsteps of a newt, but I couldn't be certain. At the glass phone booth at the front of the Gray Hare subdivision, I paused. I had never seen a real-life phone booth in the wild, only on TV and in old movies. The booth looked a little blurry from the nervous sweat getting into my eyes and clouding my vision. I needed to do something quickly, or I might not even be able to see who was after me. I spun around and kicked as hard as I could while yelling, "Eel the pain!"

Unfortunately, they didn't "eel" anything, because my kick completely missed its target. My leg kept swinging and I spun around and fell over onto my side. Sand busted up my nose as my face hit the ground.

I could hear the creature screaming . . . or was it laughing?

I rolled over and blew sand out of my nose. Standing over me and looking way too happy was Rain. He was holding on to his bike and laughing like this was all just one big laughing contest and he was determined to win.

"Why are you sneaking up on me?" I wiped my stinging eyes.

"I wasn't sneaking!" Rain insisted. "We all have places to go."

Places to go? That seemed suspicious. He probably snuck away to wash the salt water off himself. I tried to peek around him to see if he had a newt tail.

"Are you okay, Perry?"

I was a little surprised that he remembered my name.

"Can I ask you a question, Rain?"

He didn't say no.

"What's your favorite food?"

"Pizza."

Shoot. If Rain was a newt he was trying to throw me off his trail—pizza was something any real newt hated.

"You sure you don't like mealworms?"

"Good-bye, Perry."

Rain crossed the street as I sat there picking sand out of my eyes, ears, nose, and hair. After a moment, I stood up and looked around for any newt tracks or tail marks in the sand. There was nothing but sunshine and the scent of the ocean.

When I looked up the street, I couldn't see Rain anywhere. It appeared that he had just disappeared into the neighborhood. Or maybe he was hiding himself by blending into the scenery.

"Very newt-like," I whispered.

Camouflage was also squid-like, but there was no way Rain was a squid.

The Gray Hare subdivision was filled with small houses that didn't match. Some had grass roofs and peeling paint, and some were modern-looking glass boxes. A few were decorated with colorful plastic statues in their front yards or flags waving in the wind. Soon I was standing in front of what must have been my uncle's place.

"This is it."

I'll be honest, I never thought I would travel here. When Zeke told me about his home, Bunny Island had always sounded like a pretend place. Now here I was. His house looked just like I thought it would. It was small, square, and bright yellow, and it reminded me of a giant Lego brick. The multicolored shingles on the roof reflected the afternoon sun. And to my pleasant surprise, a squid was painted on the faded green front door. Zeke's garden was overgrown and he had a mailbox shaped like a pelican.

I took a deep breath and made my way up to the door with the painted squid. If only I had more in common with it than I actually did, I'd be better equipped to save my uncle. I traced my finger around the picture and then knocked three times, hoping against hope that my uncle would open it and inform me that this was all just a big misunderstanding, or that he had already escaped on his own. Then we could hang out for a bit and I could fly home, go to my room, and never get sand in my butt crack again.

Nobody answered. As I'd feared.

I reached out and turned the doorknob. The door wasn't locked, and when I pushed it open I could hear something moving around inside the house. My heart hammered in my chest. I reached into one of my still-wet pockets and pulled out a pen. Sure, it wasn't an ink blaster, but it had ink. Clutching the pen in my right hand, I prepared to jab like crazy. With my other hand, I reached down and picked up some dirt from a potted plant on the porch. Newts had sensitive eyes. A little ink and dirt to the eyes can stun them considerably.

"You can do this," I whispered. "Then again, maybe you can't."

I wasn't sure I was brave enough to walk into the house. Let's face it, I'm not a very scary opponent.

I felt like Admiral Uli when he was about to step into the Cave of Cod in *Ocean Blasterzoids* Issue #30. He had been nervous and excited to find the Kelp of Resistance. Well, I was nervous and excited to find my uncle.

I counted to five and then screamed, "It's tentacle time!"

Dashing through the door, I stumbled over a white bunny sitting in the entryway. I lurched forward onto an old leather couch that was covered with a blue knitted blanket. The blanket wrapped around my head like a warm octopus.

Valiantly, I fought it off.

It was a quick fight. When it was over, I threw the

blanket to the ground and sat up straight on the couch. The bunnies on the carpet ignored me. I wasn't surprised to see them. They seemed like just the kind of distraction a newt would use against me.

I quickly began to search the place, looking for any clue that might reveal where my uncle had been taken. Everything was a mess. Drawers were pulled open, and trash and piles of dirty clothes were scattered across the floor. A couple of bunnies chewed on chair legs and scratched at the walls. In a corner of the living room, I found a lopsided red desk.

On top of the desk sat a plastic radio shaped like a whale next to a silver picture frame. Inside the frame was a photo of my uncle and me at an amusement park in Ohio. Zeke was making bunny ears behind me. My father had taken the picture a few years ago when my uncle had come to visit us. I studied Zeke's face. He was tan and had a mustache like my dad. His eyes looked like they were lit from within, and he was smiling like always. It was a nice picture, but a lousy clue.

In the top drawer of the desk I found a small, blank *Ocean Blasterzoids* notepad.

"Perfect."

I grabbed a pen and jotted down a few known facts. Like Uli, if I was going to solve this mystery, I needed to take notes.

- *Bunny Island smells like sand and salt water: newts hate salt water.*
- *No cars, so kidnapping by: golf cart, very strong newt, ocean ship?*
- *What is Rain? Is it possible for newts to be out in the daytime? Possible to hide tail?*
- *My butt itches.*

Zeke's living room had some strange pictures hanging on the wall. There was one of a cow wearing a swimsuit and another of a big plate of scrambled eggs and pancakes. In the kitchen, a dirty pan soaked in a bucket of water on the counter, and some brown bananas sat on the counter.

I checked the ugly yellow refrigerator and found nothing but a jar of pickles and a tube of toothpaste. That didn't surprise me. My whole life, my father had stored our toothpaste in the refrigerator to keep it fresh.

I opened the freezer. It wasn't out of the question for a newt to hide weapons in ice. More than once, Admiral Uli had found newt tooters buried in the underwater snows of Mount Briny.

There was nothing in my uncle's freezer besides a bag of ice.

Inside the scratched-up old cabinets, I found some canned food and a few boxes of wheat crackers.

My father would have been glad to see that my uncle

was supporting wheat, but what got me pumped was the three boxes of baking soda I found in the last cabinet.

Newts hate baking soda! Hate it. Their slimy skin reacts poorly to it and makes it hard for them to breathe. Baking soda and ink are a newt's two biggest fears. In Issue #17, Admiral Uli takes down a whole nest of newts by gifting them an explosive, ink-grilled, baking soda–stuffed shrimp.

I took all three boxes out of the cabinet and set them on the counter. In one of the drawers, I found a plastic bag, filled it with some of the baking soda, and put it into one of my bigger pant pockets.

"This could come in handy," I said, patting the pocket.

I left the kitchen and checked out my uncle's room. He had a lumpy bed, a closet, and a beanbag in the corner. It seemed pretty normal. However, there were a lot of clothes scattered around. Either Zeke had gone somewhere in a hurry, or he had been attacked. Newts were notoriously messy. But I still didn't have any solid leads.

I glanced out the large bedroom window and into the backyard.

Zeke's big backyard was mostly filled with a garden: rows and rows of huge green plants.

On the right side of the garden stood a rusty tin shed with a wooden roof. I was staring at the shed wondering if there could be clues in there when I heard the sound of hinges whining. The hair on the back of my neck stood straight up. I thought about screaming, but Admiral Uli always says, "Why scream when you can squirt ink?"

For the record, I totally agree with Admiral Uli. Newts, along with most living creatures, hate being inked. There's one small problem—personally, my body's inkless. I've been begging my dad for an ink transplant for years, but he always says no, because he thinks it's a bad idea.

I bet he would feel differently now.

I crept out of the bedroom and could clearly hear that the whining was coming from the kitchen door. The door popped open farther.

Since I had no ink, I screamed. While I was screaming, two fat brown bunnies hopped in from the backyard.

"Sweet crab meat," I said, holding my right hand to my heart. "You two scared the squid out of me."

The bunnies didn't reply. I pulled the back door open all the way. Someone—or something—had left it ajar, and that's how the rabbits had been getting in. I walked out onto the small porch.

As I stepped down, my back foot slipped on something wet, and I flew backward. My legs shot out in front of me, and my arms waved spastically like a nerdy squid as I fell hard on my bony butt.

"Ouch!"

Whatever I had slipped on was all over the back porch. It was now also on my hands and back and butt and felt slimy and wet. I hate to jump to conclusions, but I almost always do.

"Newts!"

I jumped up and steadied myself. The surface oozed with slime. It would take much more than a couple of newts to leave the kind of mess that was coating my uncle's porch.

I got back inside, locked the door, and ran water over my hands in the kitchen sink while freaking out. Finding slime was not a comforting thing. Newts had most certainly been here. I needed more information.

I needed to call my dad.

He wouldn't have any clues, but he was waiting for my call. I double-checked the back door to make sure it was locked and then bolted from the kitchen, through the living room, and into the not-so-great outdoors.

CHAPTER SIX

A POUNDING ON THE GLASS

It took me only about ten giant steps and three impressive leaps (and two unimpressive ones) to get to the phone booth. Inside, the concrete floor was sandy. The phone itself looked old enough to be the great-grandfather of any phone that now existed.

I picked up the receiver and, using the credit card number my dad gave me, called home. It took seven rings before my father picked up.

"Hi, Dad."

"Hello, Perry. You were exactly who I was hoping would call. I'd ask how you are, but I can already hear adventure in your voice."

"Really?"

"For sure. So you arrived safely?"

"Yes," I answered.

"I miss you already. Also, do you know where you left the remote?"

"In the drawer near the footstool."

"Of course. So how's your uncle? Remember, he's a little . . ."

"Free-spirited?" I guessed.

"For sure. When we were kids he used to eat his pancakes with his hands. He'd roll them up like breadsticks and dunk them in syrup."

"I do that, too," I reminded my dad.

"Well, I suppose you two will have a great time together then," my father said with a contented-sounding sigh. "So is your uncle nearby? I'd like to talk to him."

"He's not here," I said. "I'm in the phone booth he always uses. It's just down the street from his house."

I really wanted to tell my father everything. He had always been my biggest champion, and I knew he could probably say some things that would make me feel better. But I also knew he would freak out and worry.

"How exciting," he said. "I bet the kids here in Ohio aren't getting the chance to use phone booths."

"I bet you're right."

"Soak it all in."

"I'm soaking."

"Tell me, Perry, do they have wheat on Bunny Island?"

"Yes," I said. "In fact, Zeke has wheat crackers."

"Good, I'll rest easy knowing that. Were you aware that if you chew on grains of wheat long enough they become a delicious gum?"

"Of course, but only because you've told me that my whole life."

"Wheat gum. What can't wheat do?"

It was nice to hear my dad's voice, but I had an uncle to find.

"Dad?" I asked. "When was the last time you talked to Uncle Zeke?"

"Well, I suppose it was about a month ago. He called me to tell me about some interesting carrots he was growing."

Bam, bam, bam!

Someone knocked on the phone booth. I jumped and spun around to find a girl standing on the other side of the glass smiling at me.

"Are you all right?" my dad asked. "Why are you screaming?"

"It's nothing," I said, trying to catch my breath. "I thought I saw a bug."

"You really haven't spent much time outside, have you?" He laughed. "That's why it's great you're there. Play in the sun, get a bit dirty. The almanac says this could be a big year for beneficial insects!"

The girl knocked on the glass again. This time I screamed at a lower volume.

"I should go, Dad. I'll call you tomorrow."

"Before you hang up, I need to ask you something, Perry. Didn't we go shopping for groceries a few days ago? Our kitchen cabinets are practically bare. I thought we had a whole summer supply of chips and treats."

"That's weird."

"Maybe we have mice?" my dad suggested.

"I bet that's it," I said.

The girl knocked again, and this time, it was less friendly sounding.

"I gotta go," I insisted.

I should warn you that whenever my dad calls me, we always end our phone calls by saying the same cheesy thing to each other. This time was no different:

"Go forward with wheat in your sails, Perry."

"Yes, sir, kernel."

Hey, I warned you.

I hung up the phone and opened the door of the glass booth. The girl who had been knocking shoved past me as I stepped out.

"Sorry, I . . ."

"No time," she said urgently. "So sorry."

She picked up the phone, shoved some coins into the

slot, and rapidly dialed a number.

"Come on, come on," she pleaded into the device. "Someone pick up."

I didn't usually let girls my age push me around. Actually, I had never really had the chance before.

Also, I know it's impolite to listen in to other people's conversations, but with my uncle's life in the hands of some cold-blooded newts, I needed to pay close attention to everything. Admiral Uli always insisted that those who fought injustice with him had to keep their ears open and their blowholes closed. So as the sun beat down on my neck, I eavesdropped as carefully as I could as she talked into the phone.

"What number am I?"

So, she was numbered? Maybe the number was written on her foot like the newts of Tally Island. They were all numbered because they looked alike, and it was the only way to tell them apart.

"Did I make the cut?" she asked the phone.

I could only guess what she was hoping to make the cut of—a secret academy, a spy school? Or maybe she was trying out for the Rudely-Pound-on-the-Phone-Booth team. Either way I needed to be prepared. So I reached my hand in my pocket and prepared to pull out my mask.

Things were about to go down.

CHAPTER SEVEN

SIDEKICKS AND UNLOCKED DOORS

"Argh," the girl complained as she hung up the phone. She sighed like I did whenever my comic books ended. "Dumb contest. Just once I'd like to win."

She spun around and looked at me.

She was more *cute* than *newt*. I think I might have gotten paler as all the ink drained from my face. Whoever she was, she was about my age with hair the exact same color as the popcorn I got at the movie theater near my house. Her long popcorn hair was pulled into a side ponytail that swung wildly whenever she moved. She had seriously green eyes. I'm serious. They looked brighter than Admiral Uli's underwater lawn. Her lips were covered with some sparkly junk and she was wearing a white T-shirt and a bunch of bracelets. She also had a pair of old-fashioned headphones around her neck and a bright green plastic watch on one wrist.

I slipped my mask back into my pocket.

"Sorry," the girl said as she stepped out of the phone booth. "I'm just a little upset."

There was something about her that made my head feel as if it were leaking helium. Could she be putting me under some sort of newt hypnosis? I had to know the truth. I reached into my pocket, grabbed a fistful of baking soda, and held out my powdery hand to see if she would shake it.

Not only did she shake it, but she didn't wince or dust it off or shrivel up. She was not a newt! I wanted to say something smooth and cool to her, but what came out was . . .

"I thought you were a newt."

She smiled. "A newt?" she asked. "Why would you think that?"

I could feel my cheeks glowing red. "No reason, I'm just trying to make conversation because I don't really know what to say or why I'm still talking."

"Well, that's odd. Interesting, but odd. I've never liked newts. They seem shifty."

I liked the way she talked.

"I'm Juliet Jordan," she said.

"I'm Perry Owens."

Juliet glanced at her watch. "Nice to meet you, Perry, but I've got to go."

I didn't want her to go, so I blurted out the first thing I could think of. "I might need some help. I think my uncle's house was broken into?"

"That's horrible," she said biting her lip. "You should call the police."

"Everyone knows the police are just newt agents," I explained. "Are there any secret squid agents you'd recommend around here? Preferably some that are familiar with underwater crime."

"Wow," she said with wide eyes. "This all sounds exciting. Just so you know, I've solved and figured out a few things in my life. Maybe I could help."

"You've solved things?"

"Well, not like any great mysteries, but I found my father's missing glasses, and once at the library I figured out who was taking all the pens."

"Who?"

"It was the librarian."

"Were they her pens to begin with?"

"Yes, but seriously, Perry, let me help. This island is kind of blah sometimes, and I'm not crazy about blah. I'm crazy about whatever the opposite of blah is."

"Halb?"

"Exactly! Besides, I love doing favors for people. That way, they owe me something in return. You never know when you might need some favors of your own."

"You never do," I agreed. "Okay, you can help."

"Good." Juliet smiled at me. "Now, I just need to deliver this package to Mrs. Ruth, and then I can start solving things. Come with me?"

I don't have much experience hanging out with girls or boys or humans. But for some reason, I wanted to give it a try with Juliet.

"Me go with you." My mouth was acting like an idiot.

I thought Juliet might just run away from me, but instead she said, "You say things in a weird way, but that's okay. Now come on."

We started walking toward Mrs. Ruth's house.

"So how come I've never seen you before?" she asked. "Do you live on the far side of the island?"

"No, I just came to visit my uncle."

"You did?" She was fizzing with excitement like a bottle of soda that had been shaken up. "So where are you from?"

"Ohio. And we need to walk faster."

"Wow! Ohio? I've always dreamed of going there."

"Well, I've never dreamed of coming here, but my uncle's in trouble."

"What's Ohio like?" she asked. "Do you have

computers? What about escalators? I've seen them in movies. Have you ever been on an escalator?"

I nodded. "Doesn't your mall have escalators?"

"No," Juliet said sadly. "It doesn't even have a second floor. What about music? I bet they have tons of great music in Ohio."

The only music I really liked was cephalopod whale chanting, and I didn't think that was what she was talking about.

"Uh, yeah. Totally," I said.

"Totally," Juliet echoed.

"What were you listening to?" I asked, pointing to the headphones around her neck.

"Oh, nothing," she said, turning a bit pink. "These aren't plugged into anything. I just wear them because they look cool." Juliet showed me how she put the headphone jack in her back pocket.

"It does look cool," I said.

"Thanks."

"So what was up with that phone call you had to make?"

"I was trying to win a contest," she answered. "The KBUN radio station is giving away a whole case of sugar-free gum. We don't get much gum here. Have you had a lot of gum?"

"Yeah," I bragged. "But not the sugar-free kind. It

does a number on my stomach."

"A number?"

"Two mostly."

Juliet laughed. "You're funny, Perry."

I liked having someone think that about me.

"So where are we going again?"

"I need to drop off this package to Mrs. Ruth. My mom makes homemade granola, and I deliver it to the old people on the island."

"Granola?"

"I know, it's not my favorite, but I like the old people. They have funny stories. Plus, sometimes they give me some of their old magazines."

"I like magazines because there's tons of pictures. Not that I don't like words, it's just that I'm into comics, and magazines are more comic-y than normal books." I didn't know what I was saying, and I could feel my cheeks getting red. "I'm going to stop talking now."

"You don't have to stop talking," Juliet said. "Sometimes life is better when you stop trying to make sense."

We walked between two bamboo shacks that looked more like old props from a TV show than actual places to live. Past the shacks, there was a sandy road that led to a round house with a flat, square roof. The grass in front of the house was as messy as a newt swamp. We stepped up onto the porch and Juliet knocked.

When nobody answered I said, "Maybe she's out?"

"That would be weird," Juliet said. "Mrs. Ruth has bad legs and a bad back and kind of a bad attitude. Usually, she doesn't leave her house. She just has people bring her the things she needs."

"Let *me* try knocking. I've got really solid knuckles."

I rapped on the door using a secret knock that only a follower of Uli would know. I was hoping Juliet would recognize it, but she didn't. Also, there was still no answer from Mrs. Ruth.

"I hope nothing's wrong," Juliet whispered.

Without even thinking about it, I pulled my mask out of my pocket and put it on. Juliet looked at me in shock.

"What's that?" she asked.

"It's my mask. I wear it when things get tough."

"Really?" she said, smiling.

"I know, make fun of me, everyone else does."

"Actually, I like it. It makes your blue eyes pop."

Great, now I also had to worry about popping eyes.

Juliet grabbed the doorknob and pushed it open a couple of inches.

"Mrs. Ruth!" she yelled. "It's me, Juliet."

There was still no answer, so I did my part and pushed the door open farther. The inside of Mrs. Ruth's home looked like my uncle's: a total mess. Lamps were tipped over, and there were clothes and books scattered about.

We stepped inside and searched the small house for any sign of Mrs. Ruth. Neither she nor her bad attitude were around, but the back door was open a few inches.

"I think Mrs. Ruth is missing," Juliet said.

The words caused chills to run down my spine, which I didn't like. One, because it meant I was scared, and real squids don't get scared. And two, because squids don't have spines, and feeling mine tingle reminded me that I wasn't as squid-like as I wanted to be. I got even more chills when I set my hand down on Mrs. Ruth's table and discovered that it was covered in slime.

"Unbelievable," I whispered.

While I was wiping my hand off on my pants, we both heard the front door opening. Juliet screamed and my pulse quickened as we turned to see what was coming.

CHAPTER EIGHT
QUESTION EVERYTHING AND EVERYONE

Sorry, but nobody was at the door. I thought at first that we were up against some invisible attackers, but upon further investigation I could see that it was just like at my uncle's: the door swung open due to bunnies trying to get in.

"That scared the glitter out of me," Juliet said.

"I hope I never had glitter in me."

We chased all the bunnies out of the house and then closed up Mrs. Ruth's home. Standing in the front yard, my forehead and knees began to sweat.

"What are we going to do about Mrs. Ruth?" I asked.

"Maybe she's at the doctor," Juliet suggested. "That's

the one thing she leaves her house for."

"I don't think so. Besides, my uncle's not at the doctor."

"So he's missing?"

"Yes, and I promised I would find him," I told her. "I just can't figure out why the newts would mess up my uncle's place and Mrs. Ruth's before they took them. Were they hiding something?"

"You know, newts can't mess up houses. They're small, right?"

"*Normal* newts might be."

"Does everyone in Ohio believe in things like giant newts?"

"I don't know," I said. "I don't get out much."

"Do your brothers and sisters believe in giant newts?"

"No brothers, no sisters. Just a dad."

"Where's your mom?" Juliet asked.

"She died when I was little. Or maybe . . ."

"Don't say the newts took her."

"I won't," I said. "But a real cephalopod doesn't rule out anything."

"For Salty's sake, a real what?"

For Salty's sake? I couldn't believe the words that had just come from Juliet's mouth. There was only one other person I knew who said that, and that person was Admiral Uli's girlfriend, Stacy Horse.

"What did you just say?" I asked.

"What's a cephalopod? Is it like an iPod? Because I've seen pictures of those in magazines."

"No, not that, you said something about salty."

"For Salty's sake?"

"How do you know that saying?"

"I'm not sure, but I always have," she said. " I probably got it from my mom. She says it, too."

I looked up at the blue sky expecting to see a double marinebow or some celebratory inkworks going off in the sky. Juliet definitely wasn't a newt. In fact, she was showing signs of being a squid cadet. I couldn't help but smile and breathe a sigh of relief. It felt amazing to know that there was someone here I could trust.

"Okay," I said solemnly. "Don't laugh, but my uncle and I have a deal. We promised each other that if we were ever hassled by newts, we would contact the other one. We both love the *Ocean Blasterzoids* comics, and we both know that newts are a menace that want to rid the oceans of salt water. Well, this morning I got an envelope and in it there was a card that said . . ." I pulled the card out of one of my pockets and showed it to her. It was a little bit smudged from getting wet, but still readable.

"What does it say?"

"Oh yeah, I forgot you don't speak Cephalopodian. It says help."

"Wow. So you flew out here just to help him?"

I nodded.

"And your dad is okay with that?"

I didn't answer.

"Does your dad even know?"

I kept silent.

"You came here all by yourself to help find an uncle that sent you a card with some weird scribbles on the back?"

"There was also a message chewed into the last page of the comic. It said 'MEL.'"

"I'm impressed," Juliet said.

"Don't be. Time is ticking away, and I'm no closer to finding Uncle Zeke. It's a well-known *Ocean Blasterzoids* fact that newts put on trench coats and hats and walk right up out of ponds and rivers at night to snatch their victims. Once they have them, they drag them to a cave or cove and keep them there until they have all the information they can get. After that they usually feed them to the sharks. We're lucky because with the amount of things my uncle knows, it will take the newts some time to learn everything."

"What does your uncle know?"

"He knows how to dismantle a newton bomb, for starters."

"And you believe all of this?"

"Of course."

"You're not just pulling a prank on me?"

"No way. Cross my three hearts."

"Is that a newt thing?"

"No, it's squids that have three hearts," I explained. "And two ink sacks. Newts just have a single heart and toxic skin. Now, do you know if there is a swamp or cave on this island?"

"Not that I know of. But there's a clearing near Whisker Cliffs."

"A clearing?" I asked, barely able to contain my excitement.

"What's so great about a clearing?"

I spit and sputtered for a few seconds before I could speak clearly. "What's so great about a clearing?! In *Ocean Blasterzoids* Issue #26, Admiral Uli says that clearings are perfect for land battles or holding St. Suction Day celebrations."

"St. Suction Day?"

"It's kind of like our Christmas."

"Cool."

"Can you take me there?"

"So you can celebrate . . . sucking?" Juliet asked.

"No, St. Suction Day is in March," I told her. "I need to go because there could be clues. I have a feeling about this. In Issue #23, Admiral Uli uses a clearing to gather his oxygen-breathing troops. It was there he found newt footprints that led him to the plans for their desaliniza-tion weapons."

"You have issues."

"I know, I have tons of them. I've been collecting comics for years."

"That's not what I meant."

"Well, I'm going to pretend it was," I replied. "Now lead the way, we don't have a moment to waste!"

Juliet smiled. "You're going to owe me big-time."

"If things go well, the whole world will owe both of us."

"I like that."

Juliet took off running, and I followed right behind.

CHAPTER NINE

BLURRY THOUGHTS AT THE CLEARING

It took too much walking to get to the clearing. It also took a ton of complaining about how much walking I had to do.

"My calves are burning," I said, hoping Juliet would slow down a little. "I need to find my uncle, but I also need to breathe."

"You don't get much exercise, do you?"

"Does vacuuming count? Because my dad always makes me vacuum."

"No, vacuuming doesn't count as exercise."

We pushed through thick, bird-filled palm trees, dodged a few Bunny Mooners on Segways, and hopped over hundreds of real rabbits sleeping in the shade. We walked over a couple of sandy dunes as Juliet played tour guide and I tried to pretend that walking uphill wasn't killing me.

"These little hills are called the Bunny Bumps," she explained.

"I think I can feel my lungs coming up my throat!" I explained back.

Finally, on the other side of the Bunny Bumps, I spotted the clearing.

The space was probably about the size of a football field, but to be honest I have no idea how big a football field is. I do know the exact measurements of Admiral Uli's Blowfish Ball Arena, and this clearing was similarly enormous.

In the middle of the grass, a man was riding a lawn mower. He had on large headphones, long shorts, and a sports coat. He was way too fancy looking to be mowing, and he vaguely resembled the person I had seen on the banners at the airport.

"Is that the mayor?" I asked, still attempting to catch my breath.

"Yes," Juliet replied, having already caught hers.

The clearing seemed like the perfect spot for something important to go down. The ground was flat and grassy and surrounded by thick bushes and trees.

"I forgot the mayor might be here," Juliet said. "He mows the clearing every other Monday. He might make us get off the grass or lecture us on the evils of junk food."

I sighed the kind of heavy sigh Admiral Uli did when he heard that Coral the Kid had escaped from Eelcatraz prison.

"Adults are always warning me about junk food. I wish they'd worry more about the taste of things like broccoli."

"So does this clearing look like your comics?"

"Yes and no. Mainly no, but for some reason it gives me squid pimples to look at it."

"I hope they're not painful."

"They're not. And this space does look like the right size."

"Right for what?" Juliet asked.

"To dock a newt landship," I said. "And the way it's surrounded by trees makes it private. Of course, I can't see any newts showing up while your mayor's mowing."

I started to walk around the clearing to look for any clues. Juliet followed closely behind. As we were searching, the mayor drove up on the mower and stopped right in front of us. He turned off the engine, and I could hear waves in the distance and seagulls squawking in the air. The freshly cut grass made my nose start to run.

"Well, hello, Juliet. Who have we here?"

"Perry," I answered for her.

"Hello, Perry. I'm Mayor Lapin. I don't believe I've had the chance to meet you."

The mayor climbed down off the mower and walked up to me with a large smile and an outstretched hand. He was more tanned in life than on his banners, and he had a single out-of-place tooth that stuck out and was almost hypnotizing to look at. I shook his hand while gazing at his tooth. He shook back and complimented me on my T-shirt.

"*Ocean Blasterzoids,*" he practically sang. "I remember those comics."

"You do?" I couldn't believe it! It made my heart race to know that someone here besides me and my uncle and maybe Juliet's mom was an Uli fan.

"It's been a long time, but I think I remember there was an octopus and a salamander."

"A squid and a newt," I corrected him.

"Yes, that's it. How fun to reminisce. And you say your name is Perry?"

I nodded.

"What brings you here to Bunny Island, Perry?" the mayor asked.

"I'm visiting my uncle."

"And what's your uncle's name?"

"Zeke Owens."

Both Juliet and Mayor Lapin made guffaw noises.

"Your uncle is Zeke?" Juliet asked.

I nodded.

"Zeke's a terrific person," the mayor said. "Liked by all. He's very important to this island. How is he these days?"

Juliet began to say something, but I elbowed her in the arm to shut her up. I wanted to tell the mayor that my uncle was missing, but it was too early in my investigation. It wasn't worth speaking up and having some adult try to stop me from finding my uncle. Admiral Uli never gave out more information than he had to.

"My uncle's fine," I lied.

"Good, good. Give him my best."

The mayor was wearing a green T-shirt under his sports coat with some letters written on it. I was trying to figure out what it said while he was talking. Apparently he noticed.

"Are you interested in my shirt?" he asked. "It says SOS. That stands for Sweets Are Sour."

"Wouldn't that be SAS?"

"Yes, but in the interest of making it catchy we changed the *are* to *our*. It's wordplay."

"It's wrong," I pointed out. "But whatever *ewe* want, it's not my shirt."

"The name doesn't matter that much. What's important is that we make others aware of how destructive sweets and junk food can be. I know sweet treats might be tempting, but when you pretend that sweets are sour, you can reprogram your mind."

My dad had always said that if you can't say anything nice, you shouldn't say anything at all, so I kept quiet.

"We are junk food–free and loving it here!" the mayor proclaimed.

"That's horrible," I said, ignoring my dad's advice.

"Well, it may be hard to understand, but it's for the good of the island."

"I guess I'm glad I don't live here. A life without pie and hot pockets and cheese puffs seems pretty SAD. And that stands for Sweets Are Delicious."

Juliet slapped her own forehead and checked her watch as if there might be a way for her to turn back time to the point right before I started talking. "Sorry, mayor," she apologized for me.

"Me, too," I offered. "I'm sure SOS is important or something."

"No need for either of you to apologize. I think Perry's clever. He's also an *Ocean Blasterzoids* fan, so he must be mostly good. Now, I'd love to chat longer, but I'm expected back at City Hall." He climbed onto the mower. "If you need anything in the future, just holler."

"I am a good hollerer," I told him.

Mayor Lapin reached down from the mower and

patted me on the head. Then he started the engine and drove off over the Bunny Bumps. The moment he disappeared, Juliet asked, "So, who's that guy on your shirt, anyway?"

"Admiral Uli? He's only the greatest hero ever born."

"I've never heard of him. Is he the reason you wear that glove on your face?"

"It's a mask."

"Is that something everyone from Ohio does?" Juliet asked. "Do all ten-year-olds love this Captain Oggly and wear glove masks?"

"Wait, how'd you know I was ten?"

"Just a guess."

"You don't think I could pass for eleven?"

"You look ten. Do all kids your age love Captain Oggly?"

"He's Admiral Uli, and no. Most kids aren't lucky enough to read about him."

"Oh," Juliet said. "Well, I don't know anything about Ohio. Or Uli."

"Admiral Uli lost his mom and dad when he was a baby squid," I said. "But he's got some really cool friends, Commander Cod and Stacy Horse. And enemies of course, like Figgy Newton. Plus, he has two steel-tipped tentacles, and he squirts ink to fend off newts. He fights to keep the salt in the ocean to protect the lives of all sea creatures. He can also blend into the scenery and swim as fast as a torpedo, and he's never afraid to do anything. I want to be just like that."

"It sounds like you are," she said. "I mean, you came out here to Bunny Island all by yourself. That's pretty brave."

Juliet was okay.

"I might have traveled out here alone," I said, "but at the moment I'm failing and clueless."

"That's true," a voice behind us said.

Juliet and I turned around to find Rain standing right next to us and smiling like he knew something clever.

"Hi, Rain," Juliet said coolly.

"What are you doing here?" I asked hotly. "Don't you have someone to overcharge?"

"I followed you two," he admitted. "But not for creepy reasons. I just need to find out where your uncle is."

"That's private family information."

"It's an island. Not much is private here."

"It's a big world, and not everything's known," I argued back.

Rain stared at me and looked closely at my T-shirt.

"A squid, huh? There's one of those painted on your uncle's front door."

"I'm sure Perry knows that," Juliet said.

"Whatever, squids are disgusting." Rain turned to go.

"Admiral Uli is not disgusting!" I yelled.

Rain stopped and laughed. "What is he anyway? A dumb cartoon character?"

My whole life, people have made fun of me for liking *Ocean Blasterzoids*. It didn't make sense—Admiral Uli's world was way better than reality. Now, once again, someone was giving me grief.

"Admiral Uli is more than a comic book character."

"What do you mean?" Rain asked. "Is he a toy?"

"Of course not."

"Is he a stuffed animal?"

A stuffed animal? Sure, I do have three different Admiral Uli stuffed animals back home, but Rain didn't know that. He was being a jerk, and I didn't appreciate it. I breathed in deeply and counted to ten in Cephalopodian.

"Wel, ub, loo, fran, zelp, ip, op, wuu, zin, plad."

"Are you choking?" Juliet asked.

"No, I'm fine," I said, cooling down.

"Listen, I'm not trying to be a hater. I'm just not into kiddie cartoons."

Juliet grabbed my shoulder to hold me back. She really didn't need to because Rain was bigger than me and possibly also a newt. I wasn't going to try anything without a real ink blaster or an electrified marine net. I balled up my fists and took a deep breath.

"Listen, Perry, will you just let your uncle know that I

need to talk to him?" Rain said.

"About what?" I asked.

"If you were him, I'd tell you, but you're not. So will you tell him?"

I sort of nodded.

"Good, now I'll see you two weirdos later. Oh, and don't go falling in love. Two people out in the clearing. Seems pretty romantic."

Juliet and I both began to blush violently. I felt like a boiled crab.

Rain laughed as he walked off and left us alone.

"What the . . ." I tried to start a conversation. "I mean, that's crazy. Love and everything."

"I know," Juliet said. "He's the worst."

"Well," I hemmed.

"Yeah," she hawed.

"I think maybe I'll go back to my uncle's place or call my dad again."

"Will you be okay getting back? I could help you, but my mom has more granola she wants me to deliver."

"I think I'll be fine. Squids have a great sense of direction."

Juliet slipped her nonworking headphones over her ears and waved good-bye. I followed her for a little bit and then broke off and made my way back to my temporary home.

BENEDICT TAKES THE CONTROLS

CHAPTER TEN

THE SNEAKY CARROT THIEF

By the time I got back to my uncle's house it was really late. If my dad had known I was out, walking around by myself on a strange island in the dark, he'd probably be proud . . . and then ground me.

The sky was black, but the air still felt warm and uncomfortable. Which was fitting, because my guts felt warm and uncomfortable as well. I was worried about going back to my uncle's house alone, but I didn't want to spend the night outside with the bunnies and the bugs and any rogue newts.

When I got to the house, I checked every room and closet to make sure I was alone. Then I did what most islanders didn't and locked the doors.

I dragged my snack-filled suitcases to the living room, parked them next to the couch, and went for it. I ate an entire bag of Salt & More Salt thick-cut chips, two Shock-Choc bars, a jar of marshmallow spread, and for dessert, a salted-caramel licorice rope.

The food tasted good, but I was worried about my uncle. I know I'm supposed to be strong, but sometimes even squids get down. In Issue #31, Admiral Uli cried when the Seashell Children were accidentally crushed by the Lump Whales. It took him two whole issues to clean it up and get over that.

If I didn't find my uncle soon, it would take me way more than two issues to stop hurting. I wanted Zeke to be back with me more than anything. We would probably be making rice right now and pretending soy sauce was ink. Or we would be reading old *Ocean Blasterzoids* issues together. Or making dumb promises to each other and swearing to be ink brothers forever. I was probably wrong to have come without my dad. I was in over my head.

I wanted to keep up the search, but my brain needed a few winks of sleep. The minute I put my head against the cushions, I was out. I would have slept through the night if I hadn't started dreaming about newts and taking them down with my Crab Maga skills. While I was sleep fighting, I rolled over and fell off the couch.

My shoulder collided with my suitcase, and my head bonked the ground.

"Big beefy reefs," I muttered as I sat up, rubbing my head.

For a minute, I couldn't remember if I was in Ohio or what day it was or if I was even awake. As I climbed back onto the couch, I looked into the kitchen and out one of the back windows. A long beam of white light swept across the garden.

I dropped back to the floor.

"Holy chum chunks," I whispered.

The newts had arrived! They had taken my uncle, and now they had come back for me.

I crawled around the couch and over to the window.

Something was definitely out back.

Pulling myself up, I peeked out. It should be noted that I'm an excellent peeker—it's one of my better skills.

I thought I'd see an army of newts or a great-white-shark ship, but I just saw the light. It was a single white ray, moving over the garden like the beam from a lighthouse. If it was a newt holding the light, it was only one. And he was probably from the lame part of the ocean, because it looked like he was just using a regular flashlight.

Whenever Admiral Uli has a good idea, which is often, a glowfish lights up over his head. I looked up, hoping there would be a glowing fish over mine.

Nothing lit up, but I did remember the baking soda.

I crawled to the kitchen counter, grabbed a box, and ripped off the top. Then, slowly, I inched to the back door and peered out the small window. The white light was holding steady, and there was no sign of a newt storm. I took hold of the doorknob and pushed.

A hot wind came in and filled my nose with the stench of dirt and grass.

I opened both my ears as wide as I could.

Sliiit, sliiit, rooompph.

"Newts." I managed not to shriek.

I needed to move quickly and surprise them.

I quietly slipped out the back door and tiptoed to the edge of the garden. The flashlight was now lying on the ground.

I crouched down behind the first row of vegetables.

My uncle's garden was big, filled with rows and rows of bushy growth.

Sliiit, sliiit, rooompph.

My annoying human spine tingled again.

I could hear grunting. I had never actually heard a newt grunt before, and this new experience was not pleasant. I silently recited the sacred cephalopod prayer that all squids recite when meditating in the dry caves beneath Tempura Cove:

I ink therefore I am.
Some suction is good.
What doesn't gill you makes you stronger.

I moved farther into the garden and made my way down the second row of veggies. The tall leafy greens brushed against my legs like cobwebs. Now I was mumbling the cave prayer out loud.

"Some suction is good. What doesn't gill you . . ."

My hands were shaking, and the grunting was growing louder. I saw a dark figure near the edge of the flashlight beam.

If I'm being honest, I'll admit that I wanted to run away, hop on a plane, and go home to safety. But Zeke was in trouble, and this might be my best shot at helping him.

My mind whizzed as I realized that I was about to do something incredibly stupid and brave. I only wished someone else was here to see me do it.

I took off running directly toward the shadow. I passed the flashlight on the ground and saw that the newt was holding some sort of weapon in its hands. I threw the open box of baking soda while screaming, "Calamari power!"

The box hit the newt and exploded on impact.

CHAPTER ELEVEN

A MUDDY MESSAGE

I dove to tackle the newt but didn't jump quite as far as I needed to. Instead, I hit the ground hard and rolled into its legs. The newt came crashing down on me, screaming. I reached through the cloud of baking soda to grab its ankles, but it twisted out of my grasp and hit me upside the head with its elbow.

For a newt, it had incredibly dry skin.

I could detect no slime at all, just powder, which caused it to slip from my hold and squirm away. I rolled over and picked up the flashlight and shined the light at the newt.

"Put your slimy hands in the air!" I yelled.

"What are you doing, Perry? It's me, Rain."

I stood up, keeping the light focused on him. It did look a lot like him, but he was covered in baking soda.

"Rain?" I said breathing hard. "How do I know it's really you?"

"What do you mean, 'How do I know it's really you?' I picked you up at the airport! I saw you at the clearing, you're the wad-of-cash kid!" he hollered.

"How much did you charge me for the ride from the airport?"

"Too much."

It was definitely Rain, and it seemed like he was not very happy about me throwing baking soda at him. I watched him lick the powder off his lips, and when he did . . . nothing happened.

Sadly, he was no newt.

The disappointment made my tentacles shrivel and my ink go dry. I wanted Rain to be the newt that would have answers about where my uncle was. But no, he had to be a human. I shined the flashlight directly into his eyes.

"What are you doing in my uncle's garden in the middle of the night?"

Rain squinted and held his arm up over his face. Even though he wasn't a newt, he was still suspicious.

"My mom's carrots were ruined. Her garden patch was trampled by a bunch of Bunny Mooners on Segways.

They were taking a shortcut through her garden to get to the mall. My mom can't make juice without carrots."

"Aren't there other places to get carrots?"

"Not at the moment. Everything in the juice needs to be locally grown. Only your uncle's carrot crop has come in, so I figured I'd come borrow a few."

"You mean, steal a few."

"I was going to ask your uncle, but he's not around," Rain insisted. "Listen, Perry, the people here love my mom's carrot juice. If she doesn't have it for them tomorrow, things will get ugly."

I didn't feel sorry for Rain, but I really had no need for a garden full of carrots, and my uncle wasn't around to eat them. I had been upset with Rain earlier, when he had almost killed me on his bike, but pelting him with a box of baking soda sort of made us even.

"Fine," I said. "Squids have big hearts. I guess you can take some."

"I was already planning to."

"Well, now I give you my official permission."

"Thanks for giving me permission I didn't need."

"You're welcome."

I gave Rain the flashlight to light up the carrots directly around us. The tops were so tall I didn't have to bend over to grab one.

I yanked on it, and it didn't move.

"Here," Rain said. "Use this."

Rain handed me the shovel that I had thought was a weapon. I stuck it into the ground.

Sliiit.

After I had loosened the carrot, I wrapped my arms around the leafy part and pulled upward with all my strength. The vegetable broke loose from the soil.

Rooompph!

The carrot was three feet long and as large as my leg. It was so heavy that I could barely lift it off the ground.

"That'll make a ton of juice," Rain said in awe.

I dragged the giant carrot down the row and laid it on the ground. Rain lit it up with the flashlight as we inspected it closely. When I lowered my nose, I noticed the carrot had a sort of eggy smell to it.

"Aren't carrots supposed to be orange?" I asked. "I'm not much of an expert on vegetables, but I know my colors, and that's purple."

"Maybe it's a rainbow carrot. They grow in all different colors."

"Will it still work in the juice?"

"I can't see why not."

Rain picked up the massive purple vegetable. He dusted off a spot and took a bite.

I wanted to throw up.

Rain, on the other hand, was going nuts. His eyes

went wide, and his lips curled into a gleeful smile. While chewing, he made yummy noises and groaned as tiny bits of carrot flew from his mouth.

"It can't be that good."

"It is," he insisted, still chewing. "It tastes like pizza and nacho cheese and doughnuts all smashed into one."

"Wait, that's one of my favorite combinations," I said suspiciously.

"It's amazing!" Rain continued, still spraying me with tiny bits of food as he spoke. "Try a bite."

"No way! I don't eat things pulled from the ground."

"Seriously, it's good."

"I don't believe you. I've been tricked into tasting vegetables before, and I promised myself I'd never let it happen again."

Rain took another big bite. "Unbelievable. You're missing out. I've got to get these to my mom. If you help me, I'm sure my mom will pay you something."

"I don't really need money."

"Oh, that's right. Well, if you help, I promise to never tell anyone that you were out in your uncle's garden screaming about calamari and wearing cartoon underpants. Deal?"

I looked down at my bare legs. I had completely forgotten that I had taken off my pants to sleep and not put them back on to attack the newt.

"Deal," I said.

I retrieved my pants from the house, and then the two of us pulled up a dozen carrots. I found a wheelbarrow in the tin garden shed and we filled it up.

As we walked out of the garden, I swept the flashlight slowly across the ground, making sure we didn't trip over anything. There was nothing but dirt and carrot tops and . . .

"What the eel?"

I stopped dead in my tracks. Rain stopped behind me, and one of the carrots fell out of the wheelbarrow.

"What are you doing?" he asked.

"Look."

I shined the light down. There on the ground was some sort of unusual pattern or message in the dirt.

i2NU8 EH7 E3RF

The message was stamped out perfectly. It looked like it had been made by dozens of weird little newt hands or tails.

"What is it?" Rain asked.

"I think it might be an important message." I pulled out my *Ocean Blasterzoids* notepad and quickly drew what I saw. "Yes, this is definitely something."

"Listen, Perry. When I agreed to take your carrots, I

didn't agree to stick around and stare at dirt with you."

"No, this is important."

I took out my Admiral Uli decoder glasses from one of my pockets and put them on.

"What are those?" Rain asked.

"They're tentacle spectacles. They help me decode things."

I'm pretty sure Rain was going to make fun of me, but instead he yelled, "Watch out!"

Something smacked up against my leg and then bounced into Rain's face. I dropped the flashlight and scrambled to pick it back up. Rain was yelling, and a loud piercing chirp kept sounding like an alarm clock I couldn't stop.

"Get the light!" Rain yelled. "It's biting me!"

I swung the flashlight around to point at Rain. He was on his knees, and his Rain Train T-shirt was ripped at the bottom. Also, he was holding a very large, very wriggly, gray furry blob.

"What is that?" I asked.

Rain was breathing too hard to answer.

"Is it some sort of rabbit?"

"I think so," he gasped. "But it's not like any rabbit I've seen before. It's big, but super-lightweight."

Rain turned so that I could see it better.

"Wow."

The bunny was fatter than any bunny I had ever seen. It had long gray fur and large floppy ears. It wasn't scary. In fact, it reminded me of a stuffed animal you could win at a state fair. It had big, wide eyes that looked like they had been drawn on by Disney on a sappy day, and its pink nose twitched as it stared at me.

I sort of wanted to hug it.

"Someone needs to check this thing out," Rain said. "Bunnies don't attack. They also don't look like this. We should keep it somewhere until someone can examine it."

"Let's put him in the shed," I suggested.

I helped Rain up and led the way to the shed. The inside was no bigger than a small bedroom, and it was filled with tools and old pots. Rain set the rabbit down on the dirt floor, and I slid the door closed.

"That's a really strange rabbit, right?" he asked, his breathing finally coming under control.

I nodded. "Like an adorable mutant."

"Yeah," Rain said. "Very odd. But now I need to get these carrots to the Liquid Love Shack so my mom can use them in the morning."

"And I've got a code to decipher," I said putting my tentacle spectacles back on.

Rain left without thanking me for the carrots. He also forgot to take his flashlight. I pretended like he forgot on purpose. Which was nice of him, because I used it to guide me back to the house.

I realized that it would be a perfect time for a bunch of newts to rain down and attack. I was scared, but I raised my hand to the dark sky and shouted, "I'll figure this out, Uncle Zeke!"

"I know you will," I said out of the side of my mouth, using a fake voice.

Fake Uncle Zeke was right. I knew without a doubt that I would find my uncle and save the day. Nothing would stop me. No obstacle would get in my way. No problem would stump me. I was here to succeed at all costs.

"Ouch," I said, slapping the back of my neck.

My powerful thoughts had been rudely interrupted by a mosquito bite.

"I wish I could solve the rest of this mystery indoors."

"You can't," I said, using the fake voice again.

The truth, like the mosquito bite, stung.

CHAPTER TWELVE
ROOTING FOR ROOT VEGETABLES

I tried for almost an hour to figure out what the code in the dirt meant. For some weird reason, my tentacle spectacles were no help—they just made everything rose-colored. Eventually, I became too sleepy to go on, so I went into my uncle's bedroom and passed out on his bed.

The plan was to sleep for just a couple of hours, but I was so exhausted that I didn't wake up until lunchtime the next day. I shot out of bed, panicked about the time I had lost. Quickly, I took a shower and ate two bags of Get-a-Load-of-Salt chips and a box of peanut butter gummi bears. I decided to comb my hair in case I ran into anyone, like Juliet, and while combing it I remembered . . .

"The rabbit!"

I grabbed a bowl of water, some pickles from the refrigerator, and a handful of wheat crackers and took them out to the shed. The big gray bunny was sleeping in the corner, huddled up so that he looked like a hairy beach ball. He was even cuter asleep. I had to fight the urge to pick him up and rock him in my arms while whispering baby talk into his silky ears. His nose twitched, and I could have sworn he was humming as he slept. The amount of adorable was almost too much to handle. This was no normal bunny. I carefully set down the water and food, backed away, and closed the door.

Bunnies this adorable *had* to be in cahoots with the newts.

On my way back into the house, I racked my brain, trying to think of any mention of bunnies in *Ocean Blasterzoids*. I couldn't remember a single one, although I still hadn't read all of Uli's adventures. Maybe in one of the issues I hadn't read yet, the newts had ray guns that made normal bunnies look like they had just popped out of some highly imaginative and upbeat child's dream.

My deep thought was interrupted by a knock at the door. Rain stood on the front step. He looked tired. His shirt was ripped, his shorts were dirty, and his eyes were a bit glossed over.

"Are you okay?" I asked. "You've got the pupils of a terrified tuna."

"Fine, I'm just a little exhausted. I need some more carrots, and I need them now. The locals are going crazy for this juice—crazy. The mayor has come by, like, five times. My mom is swamped. And to make things worse, two of her workers didn't show up today."

"She's got workers missing?"

"Yes," Rain insisted. "So now I have to help pick up the slack. Your uncle grew some amazing carrots. Is he here now?"

"No," I said nervously. "He's doing some sort of grown-up thing—filing taxes or buying vitamins. I don't know." I didn't want to lie to Rain any longer, but I couldn't risk him telling an adult who would put an end to me living unsupervised.

Rain didn't seem to care. "Well then, could you help me?"

"Me?"

"Yeah," he pleaded. "We need more carrots, and you were pretty good at digging them up last night."

"Really?" I said. It sounded nice when someone besides my dad or uncle told me I was good at something.

"I'm supposed to find Juliet to get her to help me with . . . a thing."

"Juliet's helping at the Love Shack, too."

Knowing Juliet was there made it much easier for me to be charitable.

"Okay," I said, looking at my arms. "Let's put these tentacles to work."

As we were digging up the carrots, I saw Rain lick a couple of them, even though they were still covered in dirt, while he was stacking them in the wheelbarrow.

"These things are so good," he said.

I shuddered. "It makes me sick just to look at them."

As soon as the wheelbarrow was filled to overflowing, Rain instructed me to grab one of the handles to help him push.

"Wouldn't it be easier if you just pushed it yourself?" I asked.

"I thought you wanted to work out your tentacles."

Reluctantly I grabbed one of the handles as Rain grabbed the other.

"Push hard!" he ordered.

This was not part of my plan. I had not flown to Bunny Island to push wheelbarrows. I had flown here to rescue my uncle. And now Rain was making me do manual labor.

"Harder," Rain said. "And run. My mom's probably already out of juice."

I dialed up my inner squid and pushed as hard as I could.

CHAPTER THIRTEEN

BLEND FOR YOUR LIFE

I was pretty mad at Rain. For some reason, when I got tired of pushing, he refused to stop and let me ride on top of the carrot-filled wheelbarrow.

"Pleeeease!"

"Stop complaining, and push harder," he yelled. "We're almost there."

Just when I thought I could whine no more, I saw the Liquid Love Shack in the distance. It looked like every local was in line waiting for juice. We ran past the line and to the back door of the shack. Rain pulled it open, and there was Juliet.

"Perry," she said. "Are you here to help Flower?"

"Flour what?" I asked.

"No," she replied. "Flower is Rain's mom. A couple of her workers didn't show up."

"Don't you think that's weird?" I asked. "People missing and not showing up?"

"It's not that unusual," Rain said. "People are pretty laid-back around here. And some folks leave the island now and then to go to the mainland. Now come on and help me unload these carrots."

We dumped the carrots inside the door, and Juliet and I began carrying them over to the row of blenders along the far wall. Rain's mom was at the counter, filling orders as a few long-haired workers were blending carrots at high speed.

"This is nuts," I yelled over the buzz of blenders. "All this for vegetable juice?"

I handed a large carrot to a man with a gray ponytail. He grabbed it and instantly began peeling and chopping. Meanwhile, Flower kept calling out the orders.

"Two tickle-sized, three wink, and one great karma–sized!" she yelled.

Despite her weird drink names, I liked Flower right away. She was probably my uncle's age. She had warm brown skin and long black hair that flipped upward at the ends. She was as skinny as a post and as pretty as someone standing in a flowery field, petting a horse on a sunny day. Her smile suggested she was having a good time, even though she was serving carrot juice that smelled like eggs.

She spotted me and dropped what she was doing to run right over.

"You must be Perry."

I nodded.

"Thank you so much," she said. "I don't know how Zeke grew these, but they're marvelous. Do you think you could help out by peeling a few?"

That sounded horrible, but I nodded again.

She handed me a peeler and told me to copy what Juliet was doing. The blenders were buzzing, the customers were shouting, but Juliet was smiling and peeling.

"Hold the carrot with the tip facing down," she said. "Then slide the peeler away from you with a quick stroke."

I picked up a large purple carrot and tried to copy her.

"Did they find Mrs. Ruth?" I yelled to Juliet over the noise of the blenders.

"No, but I found out that there's a health retreat happening on the far side of the island," she said. "Big companies put them on and everyone goes and stares at the sun and sweats out their problems. I think she might have gone there. Maybe your uncle's there, too."

"He's not," I insisted. "He's in trouble, and I really shouldn't be here peeling carrots. I should be looking for him."

I finished peeling my first carrot, and it didn't look good.

"Try harder on the next one," Juliet said. She then began peeling carrots like a mad person. I tried to keep up so that she didn't outpeel me, but she was way too fast.

I was doing such a poor job that Flower moved me up to the counter to help hand the customers their drinks. I was okay with the move because it was the perfect place to get information. As I handed out the cups, I was able to ask all sorts of questions.

"Do you know my uncle Zeke?"

"Do you know anything about 'MEL'?"

"How do you feel about amphibians?"

"Have you seen anyone wearing trench coats lately?"

"Are you aware of any coves or caves?"

"How can you drink this stuff?"

Surprisingly, the customers had no problem answering all the questions I threw at them.

"Yes, we know Zeke."

"I have a cousin named Mel who lives in New York."

"Amphibians are fine."

"No trench coats, but I did see a lady wearing a windbreaker."

"There are caves on the other side of the island."

"Easy! This juice tastes like heaven."

The blenders kept on blending, the customers kept

on ordering, and I kept asking questions. Nobody had specific information about my uncle, but everyone seemed to know him and most thought he was probably at the retreat. My mind was filled with useless information, and before I knew it, it was eight o'clock at night and Flower was shutting down for the day. She had to turn the last few people away.

"More juice tomorrow!" she called out.

People groaned and complained, but eventually they walked away, leaving the inside of the Liquid Love Shack much quieter.

All of us workers were covered with bits of carrot and splashes of juice. Juliet had a long, fluffy green carrot leaf in her hair, and everyone's hands were purple.

"Gather round," Flower said.

We did, and she poured everyone—besides me—a glass of the juice. She tried to give me some, but I settled for water.

"Thank you," Flower said, raising her glass. "In all the years I've run the Liquid Love Shack, we have never had a day like today. And it wouldn't have been possible without Perry."

I looked around, thinking she was talking about some other Perry. It took me a moment to realize she meant me.

Flower lifted her glass higher. "To Perry and Zeke

and their miraculous carrots."

"To Perry," everyone cheered.

"To me," I said holding up my glass of water.

I wasn't trying to make a joke, but everyone laughed. I took a drink of water as Flower turned on the radio and music played. We all sat around and ate sandwiches and drank juice and water. It would have been my best day ever . . . if not for the fact that I still hadn't found my uncle. He was counting on me and I was wasting time celebrating his carrots.

As I was sitting there worrying, Rain approached me.

"Listen, you're not the worst Bunny Mooner ever."

"Thanks."

"I mean, you're a bit unusual, but you really helped my mom." Rain smiled a weird smile and punched me in the shoulder with a purple fist. "Later," he said, walking off.

The moment Rain left, Juliet came over and sat down. She had her headphones around her neck, and her purple hands looked almost like cool superhero gloves.

"You feel all right?" she asked.

"Yeah, but it's hard to be too pumped up when I still haven't found my uncle."

"I'm sure he's at the retreat."

"Are you kidding?" I asked. "I know he's not."

"Think about it, Perry. No newts took him."

"What?"

"That's really not possible. I borrowed an encyclopedia from one of the granola people, and there are no newts that grow anywhere near big enough to kidnap your uncle."

I couldn't believe what I was hearing. At first I thought Juliet was teasing me, but she just kept talking.

"I like things to be mysterious, too, but I think it's safe to say that your uncle is just on vacation or something."

"That, that is the most unsafe thing to say I've ever heard," I sputtered.

"I'm not trying to make you mad." She was beginning to sound a little bothered herself. "But there's got to be a logical explanation."

If I hadn't already tested Juliet for newt, I would have sworn she was one. She was talking crazy. A logical explanation? That was nuts, and I was too tired and upset to hear any more.

"Stop," I said. "You don't understand. There were messages in the comic book he sent me. One said 'MEL,' and 'mel' means *newt*."

"You don't know that. It could stand for something else completely. Maybe he meant caraMEL."

"He didn't mean that."

"Then it could have just been a joke, Perry. You do realize the comic squid guy isn't actually real, don't you? You should stop wasting your time worrying about imaginary newts and, you know, enjoy the island. No one's going to take the salt from the water."

My breath popped out of my mouth as if I had been punched. I had thought that Juliet was on my side. I had thought she was a friend. Now I just thought she was being mean.

"I've gotta go," I said.

"Perry—"

Juliet's words were interrupted by a knock on the back door of the Liquid Love Shack.

When Flower opened the door, there was Mayor Lapin. He had come to congratulate her on having such a big day.

"I love to see business booming here on Bunny Island," he said.

Flower invited him in, and everybody continued to drink and celebrate.

But not me.

I slipped away and headed back to my uncle's house. My stomach felt like it was housing two badgers who were now fighting over a wad of meat. Juliet had bailed on me. Once again, I was my uncle's only hope. Unless I picked up the pace, he was never going to be rescued.

As much as I hated to do it, I started to run. I had some very important things to do and no time to waste.

CHAPTER FOURTEEN

COMING THROUGH LOUD AND FEAR

As soon as I got back to my uncle's house, I sat down at the small red desk, took out my notepad, and quickly listed some of the latest leads.

- *Find out about the health retreat.*
- *There's a cave on the other side of the island.*
- *Could 'MEL' stand for caraMEL?*

I paced around the living room, trying to figure out what to do next and wondering how Admiral Uli would handle this situation. I splashed some cold salt water on my face, which sometimes helps me feel more squid-like, and ate a bag of Salted Beef Chunkies. They almost didn't taste good, thanks to my current worry level.

As I swallowed my last bite, I heard banging coming from the backyard. It startled me at first, but then I remembered that Rain was going to come for more carrots. Still, I held my pen in my right hand like a weapon and grabbed the flashlight with my left.

Looking out the small window on the back door, I couldn't see anything but a dark garden.

Bang! Bang!

The noise was metallic sounding, like something pounding against tin. I saw no lights or newts, so I slowly opened the door and slipped out.

Bang! Bang! Crash!

"Who's there?" I yelled out. "I've got a pen!"

Bang! Crash!

The noise was coming from the shed.

"The bunny," I whispered.

I went back inside and grabbed some wheat crackers and a large glass of water.

Bang! Bang! Bang!

"I'm coming!" I yelled as I ran to the shed. "Hold your paws."

Bang! Bang!

I slid open the door and prepared to pour water into the dish I had put in there earlier. But even with all my squid training, the bunny was faster than me.

The rabbit sprang out of the darkness and smacked me right in the chest. I flew backward onto my butt and spilled water down my shirt. The bunny screeched and sprang into the garden.

"Wait!" I yelled. "Come back!"

I picked myself up and tried to find the rabbit, but there was no sign of it, and the night was too dark.

"Soft clammy oysters!" I cursed.

I went back inside and sat down at the desk. I turned on my uncle's plastic whale radio, and the soft sounds of the radio station filled the room. It wasn't my favorite music, but it was nice to have some noise in the room. I flipped through my notepad to find the code I had seen in the dirt the night before. I put my Admiral Uli tentacle spectacles back on and even tried squinting to see if that would help.

It didn't.

I stared cross-eyed at the message. That didn't work either. I held my eyes open really wide with my fingers and stared. That worked even less.

I needed my uncle. He was a master at secret codes. He would be the perfect person to save himself, if only he was here to help me do so.

While I was gazing at the message, my once-wide eyes began to slowly drift shut, and my head started to nod. I folded my arms and rested them on the desk.

Then I laid my head on my arms to see if that felt more comfortable. I guess it did, because I fell asleep instantly.

While I snored and drooled, the radio station signed off for the day and stopped playing music. After two low beeps, the bothersome sound of static filled the room. With my eyes still closed, I reached out and slapped the whale radio to shut it off. It tumbled from the desk and hit the floor. For a moment the room was quiet, but as I shifted my head on my folded arms, I heard static again. It hummed and popped until it was just annoying enough to make me raise my head and open my eyes.

I blinked and glanced down at the radio on the floor. The static buzzed and hissed, and I thought I could hear some words forming in the noise.

"Suren . . . duny . . . who . . . man."

I gasped and yawned at the same time, which caused me to awkwardly burp.

The static continued to pop and hiss, and as I was reaching down to turn it off I heard the words again.

"Suren . . . duny . . . who . . . man."

I had no idea what it meant. It might have been Cephalopodian or Newtian or any other language. It sort of sounded like "surrender, puny human," which made chills shoot around my body like I was undergoing eelectric-shock therapy. After all, *I* was a puny human!

I grabbed the radio and held it up to my ear.

There was nothing but static.

"This place is crazy," I said, turning it off. "I must be hearing things."

I set the radio on the desk and decided to go sleep on a bed instead of in a desk chair. As I was standing up I heard . . .

"Suren . . . duny . . . who . . . man."

I looked at the radio. It was off, but noises were still coming from it. I grabbed the wire to unplug it and saw that the wire was frayed and torn in two different spots. I reached for the outlet and pulled the plug.

The radio fell silent.

I sat in the chair, too scared to get up, waiting to see if the radio would speak again.

Whap, whap, whap!!

There was a loud banging on the front door. I was looking for a weapon or at least my pen, when Rain and Juliet came crashing into the house. They didn't look exactly like I remembered.

"What are you doing?" I yelled. I was still mad at Juliet for her ridiculous suggestion that I should ignore the newt threat.

"Something's happening, Perry," she cried. "Something strange. Look at us."

Juliet had fur on her arms and legs, and her nose seemed smaller and kind of twitchy. Her green eyes were squinted, and her lips were no longer shiny. Rain was also furry, and his eyes were pulsating.

"Thick seafood gumbo," I said stepping back. "What's going on?"

"We don't know," Juliet wailed. "But we wanted to see if you were all right? Whatever is happening is happening to a bunch of people. Some sort of allergic reaction. Mayor Lapin is freaking out. Something is going on with our island."

"I know," I shouted. "My uncle's radio has messed-up wires, but still the static said 'surrender, puny human.'"

Rain gasped. "You're a puny human!"

"I know," I had to admit.

"What's happening?" Juliet moaned. "If it's allergies, it's the worst case this island has ever seen. It's like we're all turning into—BUNNY!"

Juliet pointed to the front window as a hairy blob broke through the glass and bounded into the room. I covered my eyes to protect them. When the sound of falling glass stopped, I dropped my hands.

There, on the floor, shimmering in the glass dust and twitching its nose, was the very same rabbit who had gotten away earlier. The creature stood on its hind legs and made an . . . adorable expression.

"Awww," Juliet said. "It's so cute!"

"I know," I agreed. "Maybe we should hug it."

"Look at its long fur," she said. "Do you have a brush I could borrow? I need to brush it this instant."

"I'm more of a comb person," I said, reminding myself that I wasn't even supposed to be talking to Juliet.

Rain was staring at the bunny in a sort of trance. "Let's call him Sir Softy."

"Ohhhhh," Juliet cried. "Sir Softy."

"Wait a second!" I said. "Don't you see? We're falling under some strange newt spell that makes us really, really like bunnies. The newts probably want to lull us into a dazed condition so they can begin their master plan of taking all the salt out of the ocean and going fresh. Just think of how many creatures will die if the water is changed—millions and millions of squids alone!"

Sir Softy squeaked and wiggled its pink nose.

"Ohhh," Rain cooed. "That's the cutest thing I've ever seen."

"You're not listening—millions of squids will die. Besides, that bunny tried to attack us last night," I reminded him. "And now it just broke through a glass window. I think it needs to be captured, not adored. I should find a net."

The bunny shook its head.

"Did you see that?" I asked. "I think it's trying to communicate."

"Ask it a question," Rain said.

"Are you telling us something?" I asked the bunny.

It nodded its head and lifted its right paw to make a waving motion.

"I need a camera," Juliet insisted. "I've got to take some pictures."

"I don't have a camera."

"I could try to draw a picture of it," Rain offered.

"Would you?" Juliet asked, clapping her hands with glee.

Sir Softy waved his paw again, and I have to say, it melted my three steely squid hearts.

"Wait," I said. "Maybe Sir Softy's waving because it wants us to follow him."

The rabbit bobbed its big furry head up and down. His ears bounced wildly, and his wide eyes looked alive and shiny.

"You do want us to follow you?" I asked.

More nodding.

"Then lead the way!"

The fat gray bunny moved to the front door, and I pushed it open. The bunny hopped out and instantly took off.

"Come on!" I waved to Juliet and Rain.

We all chased Sir Softy, who bounced like a big furry ball down the street and past the glass phone booth. With ten large hops, the bunny crossed the beach and was on to Rabbit Road. Dawn hadn't come yet, but under the small lights lining the road, I could see a few locals stumbling around. Several of them seemed to have the same condition as Juliet and Rain; I spotted bunny ears and large teeth and patches of fur on arms and legs. The bunny-people were clustering in herds and emitting weird squeaking noises.

Sir Softy almost knocked over a woman with a fuzzy face, who was hopping around and scrunching her nose.

She squeaked meanly at us as we ran past.

Sir Softy crossed the street and headed toward the Bunny Bumps. I was tired and more than just a little unhappy about all the outdoor running and walking I had been doing lately. Juliet and Rain seemed tired and more than just a little unhappy about having furry arms. Their running style was more awkward than mine—they were hop-scurry-skipping.

"Are you guys all right?" I yelled. "Do you need to stop and rest?!"

"No," Juliet yelled back.

"Please!"

"No," Rain insisted.

When we reached the Bunny Bumps, my thighs were burning. When we reached the clearing, my thighs, legs, stomach, and butt were on fire. And when we reached the center of the clearing, Sir Softy stopped and I gladly did the same. I bent over and put my hands on my knees while taking in big gulps of warm, salty island air.

"Why are we here?" Juliet asked in confusion.

I just kept taking big breaths.

"I feel really uncool right now," Rain said with concern. "I think karma's getting me back for all the stuff I've done. I mean, something's really happening to me."

"You think?" Juliet said sarcastically. "I know something's happening to you. You have fur all over, and your nose is shrinking."

"Not my nose," Rain said touching it. "It's one of my best features!"

"That might be the least of your worries," I finally spoke. "Look."

I pointed to the vegetation at the edge of the clearing. Sir Softy chirped and chattered.

"Uh-oh," I whispered.

Something was coming from the bushes.

CHAPTER FIFTEEN

THE LOST BUNNIES

After one of us screamed, and it's not important to say who, dozens of fluffy bunnies emerged from the bushes and moved toward us. They were standing on their hind legs, and even in the dim early morning light, I could see that they were oversize and . . . well, super-duper adorable.

It probably wasn't necessary for whoever screamed to have done so.

The rabbits all looked a lot like Sir Softy. They had big wide eyes and round faces that were surrounded by thick, flowing fur and topped with long, soft-looking ears. Their whiskers twitched as they scrunched their noses and smiled.

"I don't know if I should be worried or delighted," Juliet whispered.

"Maybe you should look in an encyclopedia to find out how you feel," I said. I was still a little annoyed with her for everything she'd said back at the juice shack, but it was hard to stay angry with someone who looked as ridiculous as she did.

Juliet ignored my comment. Rain just twitched.

Sir Softy stood on his back legs and stretched out his front paws. He motioned to the other bunnies, and all of them began to squeak and stumble closer to us.

My first thought was to run. My second thought was to not run, because my legs were spent. My third thought was to prove my theory that the horrible newts were distracting everyone with the adorable bunnies. Amphibian evil was nearby. I could feel it in every bit of my cartilage.

The animals shuffled forward until they were all directly in front of us. It looked like a gathering of every cute thing I had ever seen on the internet.

The bunnies all began to hop and jump with excitement.

"What are they trying to tell us?" Rain asked. "It would really help if they could talk."

"Wait a second!" I got out my notepad and flipped through the pages. When I found the one with the message I had copied from the dirt, I tore it out and handed it to Juliet. "The bunnies can't talk, but I think they stamped this out. At first I thought it was newt tails, but under the circumstances, bunny feet seem more likely. I haven't figured out what it says yet. It looks like it's written using the newt amphibianabet."

"The amphibianabet?" Juliet asked.

"It's like the amphibian alphabet."

She took the torn page from me as the bunnies circled us and twitched their ears. She stared intently at the page.

i2NU8 EH7 E3RF

"I don't know what it says," she admitted. "It could be anything."

As Juliet was holding the message, I could see it from behind, and I realized the mistake I had made. I took the page back and stared at the writing. Flipping the paper over I looked at it from the back side.

"What are you doing?" she asked.

"I was looking at it wrong."

I showed Juliet and Rain the back side of the page. The ink had bled through, and the words were upside down and *reversed*. I could clearly see that it said:

FREE THE BUNS!

"Whoa, that's deep," Rain said, confused. "Are they talking about *buns* like the ones we sit on? Free the butts? Are they against pants?"

"No," I said with excitement. "*Buns* means 'bunnies.' Don't you see? The scratching rabbits, the carrots, the transformations, you being attacked in my backyard, that was just the rabbits trying to warn us about something. And why did my uncle send me a cry for help?"

A glowfish lit up over my head.

"Wait a fathom," I said while looking at Sir Softy. "I don't think these are regular bunnies."

Rain squeaked.

"What I'm saying is that if a squid can be an admiral, then it's not a stretch to think that carrots could be cursed or an uncle could become a rabbit . . . and look at that yellow one. The way it moves. I think it has bad legs and a bad back."

"Mrs. Ruth?" Juliet exclaimed.

The yellow bunny shook its fur and chirped.

I had no problem with people turning into bunnies. In *Ocean Blasterzoids* Issue #73, Admiral Uli was turned into a sea cucumber for the whole story. It was actually one of my least favorite issues because he just lay around on the bottom of the ocean floor the entire time.

"Reeeeeeeeeeeech!"

I looked down to see Sir Softy standing right in front

of me. He was gazing up and keeping perfectly still. He blinked his big eyes, and for the first time I noticed that the fur over his mouth was brown and looked a little bit like a mustache. My heart pounded, and my palms got even sweatier than the run to the clearing had made them.

It couldn't be.

I wiped my palms on the side of my green cargo pants and gulped. There was only one way to know for sure.

I made a *V* on each hand with my two main fingers. I then stuck out my arms and crossed them at the wrists to make the sign of the squid. I held my breath as Sir Softy looked up at me.

All eyes were on us.

Sir Softy stretched his front legs and crossed them. Then with his furry paws, he took hold of my hands and shook them both sideways.

"Ohhhhh," Juliet and Rain said in unison.

There was no mistaking the secret handshake of Admiral Uli.

"Uncle Zeke?" I gasped.

Sir Softy—I mean, Zeke—nodded and let go of my hands. I stepped back and looked at him.

"It really is you?"

He nodded again.

I couldn't help myself. I shouted "hooray" in Cephalopodian.

"Zelt, Zelt, Pod!"

I had found my uncle! Well, kind of. I picked him up and looked at him closely. "Are you okay?"

"Don't be crazy," Rain said. "Rabbits can't talk."

"Right," Juliet said. "That's the crazy part of all this."

I held my uncle in my right arm, and he began to nibble on my fingers. His fur was incredibly soft.

"Ahhh," Juliet said. "That's darling."

"It is," I agreed. "But how did this happen?"

A brown rabbit with a wild tuft of hair on top of its head handed a purple carrot to Sir Softy. Sir Softy in turn reached out and tried to give it to me.

"No, thanks," I said.

"I'll take it," Rain offered. "Waste not, want not." He grabbed the carrot and took a big bite.

All the bunnies shivered as Rain bit down. There was a popping noise followed by a bunny ear springing out of his bleached hair. The ear grew like a weed until it was six inches long and floppy. It hung in front of Rain's left eye, making him look like a troubled bunny boy.

"Of course," I whispered.

"That's not a normal allergic reaction," Juliet whispered.

Rain reached up and grabbed his new ear. "Um . . . I don't think that should be there."

The rabbits squeaked and stamped their little feet

like an army of Easter mascots, chanting what sounded like, "Reets, reets, reets."

"Don't you see what's happening?" I said. "It's the carreets! The carreets are turning the whole town into ... something odd."

"So it's just the carrots?" Juliet asked. "What about the 'surrender, puny human'?"

"It must have been some newts just messing with me." I said angrily. "They're like that. How could I be so stupid? Or I could have heard things wrong. Occasionally, that happens."

Rain raised his hand.

"Do you have a question?" I asked.

"Um, yes. I've eaten a lot of those carrots, and Juliet has had a couple, too. Actually, by now most of the locals have probably drunk a bunch of them."

"That's not a question," I pointed out. "That's a statement. But we've got to do something before you're all permanently adorable. There has to be a cure or an antidote of some sort. We also need to stop people from eating any more of those carrots. We should warn the town."

"It's really early," Juliet said. "Do we wake everyone up?"

Just then, a piercing alarm filled the air and began doing just that.

CHAPTER SIXTEEN

CALLED TO THE MALL

The wailing alarm filled the air as people poured out of their homes, and frantic hordes of wild bunnies scattered in all directions. The megaphones on top of the streetlights continued screeching loudly.

"What's happening?" I yelled.

"It's the Emergency Bunny System," Juliet yelled back. "It's supposed to warn us of tidal waves."

"All I see is an avalanche of rabbits and strange-looking people! Should we . . ."

The alarms abruptly stopped and a computer-generated voice began speaking through the megaphones.

"This is the Emergency Bunny System. All Bunny Island locals should report to the mall immediately for instruction. Visitors go on about your business. That is all."

"This could help," I said to Juliet and Rain. "If everyone's at the mall, we can go there and warn them all about the carrots."

"Good," Rain said, thumping one fur-covered foot as he spoke. He had lost his shoes somewhere along the way as his feet changed shape.

Holding my uncle, I looked down at the other mutant bunnies in the clearing. They all stared up at me as if they were expecting me to say something wise. The bunny-people were right. It was time for an inspiring speech.

"Hold on," I told them.

I motioned for Juliet and Rain to gather around me. I set my uncle on the ground, and the three of us huddled over him to have a private conversation. We put our arms over one another's shoulders and looked down at Zeke.

"Why are we doing this?" Rain asked, keeping his voice down.

"It's an *Ocean Blasterzoids* thing," I explained. "It's kind of like a bubble huddle, and yes, it would work better if we all had tentacles or fins and were underwater. But I've never been able to do one before because it was just me. So this is a good moment. Even though some of us are becoming giant bunnies. Now we're a team."

"We're a team?" Juliet asked. "What's our name?"

"I don't think we need a name," I explained. "We're just in this together. Now, let's get to the mall and see what we can do to save this island."

"How about Team Solution?" Juliet suggested.

"Like I said, we don't need a name," I said. "Let's just get to the mall and warn everyone about the carrots."

"Should we do something with the mutant bunnies?" Rain asked.

"Not now. They should stay here," I said. "It's probably safer. Also, they might help us later. Admiral Uli always has a backup team in case of surprise danger. It's like Issue #12 when he used a gang of flounders to defeat some rogue anemones. Now let's do this. One, two, three . . . break!"

Rain was the only one who clapped, but we broke up the bubble huddle and turned to face the lost bunnies.

"You should all wait here," I said loudly. "We'll come for you as soon as possible. You should know, I've read a lot of comics, and if they've taught me anything, it's that for every ink stain, there's a stain remover, and for every messed-up carrot, there's an antidote. We will find the answer and come back to save you all."

The mutant bunnies tried to clap, but their soft, furry paws just made a quiet, wispy noise.

"Great speech," Rain said. "Now, let's get moving."

There was no way I was going to leave my uncle

behind, so when we took off running, I picked him up and took him with us.

Rabbit Road was filled with juiced-up locals. They all looked hairier and more bucktoothed than usual. Some had rabbit ears, and some had whiskers. All of them were clumsily hopping their way to the mall. I also saw some Bunny Mooners on Segways staring at the commotion in disgust and complaining about how out of shape and hairy everyone looked. Apparently, they didn't care about the problems happening on the island.

"I'm changing even more!" Juliet yelled as she ran. "Look at me!"

Juliet had fur on her knees and forearms, and one of her ears was a full-on bunny ear now.

"How bad is it?" she asked.

"It's not bad," I lied. "You look like the rest of the locals."

"This is horrible," she cried. "I don't want to be a bunny. How will my headphones fit with bunny ears?"

"Let's just get to the mall and tell everyone to stop drinking purple juice." I panted before continuing. "Then we can figure out how to change you guys back."

"Has anything like this ever happened in Ohio?" Juliet asked.

"I wouldn't know. I hardly ever leave my house."

"Weird," Juliet said. "You seem to do well outdoors."

I wished my dad were here to hear that. I also wished he was here because I could use his help. Sure, *The Old Farmer's Almanac* didn't have a chapter on cursed carrots and rabbit people, but it would have helped just to have him around.

When we got to the trees next to the Bunny Island mall, I stopped running. I looked behind me and saw that all the lost bunnies had followed us, even though I'd told them not to.

They were now finding hiding spots in the trees and bushes. Their big fearful eyes told me they only wanted to help.

"Hey, mutant bunnies," I said. "Can you wait here? Once we know what's happening, I promise we'll come get you."

They seemed okay with that. I held on to my uncle, Sir Softy.

Juliet, Rain, Sir Softy, and I walked out of the trees and into the mall parking lot. There were hundreds of people who looked like half rabbits entering through the front doors of the mall. Everyone was talking loudly and acting confused.

A couple of men from the mayor's staff, wearing red T-shirts that said BIRP, were ushering people into the mall, rushing the crowd along.

My friends and my uncle and I fell into the line of

half-bunny mutants moving through the doors.

Inside, other staff members in red T-shirts were directing everyone into the food court. Since it was still early morning, all the restaurants were closed. In the middle of the seating area stood a large indoor fountain with a statue of a rabbit with angel wings, spitting water into the air.

The mayor's staff was directing people to sit at the metal tables and chairs around the fountain and handing out muffins and water.

Mayor Lapin stood near the fountain, wearing a white apron. He was helping an old woman . . . actually, it might have been a half-bunny human . . . well, the important thing is that the mayor was helping some sort of creature sit down and have a muffin. He was bustling around, patting people on the ears and trying to make everyone feel comfortable despite this terrible situation.

I looked around at the rest of the dark, empty mall— only the food court had any lights on.

The muffins that the BIRP men were passing out must have been good, because everyone was going crazy over them. The room was full of the sounds of bucktoothed chewing. Obviously, the locals were all stress eaters.

"Maybe we should eat something, too," Juliet suggested.

"No way," I said. "I don't like muffins. It's too easy for

grown-ups to hide healthy things inside them. Besides, there isn't time to eat. We have to get to the mayor. He needs to know about the carrots."

Holding my uncle, I tried to push my way through the crowd. Before I got much closer, I heard a loud, metallic screech coming from a microphone. I plugged my normal ears while everyone else plugged their mutating ones. I looked up and saw that Mayor Lapin was holding a mic and standing on the edge of the angel rabbit fountain.

"Attention," he said. "Attention, please. This is a most trying time. By now you all know that there is something mysterious happening on our island. There seems to be a virus going around."

Some people were listening, but a lot of them were too busy chowing down on muffins to pay full attention. I looked at Juliet. She had a muffin in each hand. She stared at them lovingly and then took a big bite out of one of them.

My tentacles began to tingle as my suction sense kicked in—something wasn't right.

"Don't worry," the mayor announced. "I will get everything under control, or my name isn't Mayor Erwin Lapin."

Mayor Erwin Lapin? My uncle wasn't trying to warn me against newts, he was warning me about MEL— Mayor Erwin Lapin!

I glanced around quickly. The only normal-looking humans in sight were me, the mayor, and his staff. Everyone else was in various stages of mutation. He was playing everyone for a fool. I turned to Juliet.

"These muffins smell amazing," she cooed.

My tentacles tingled like mad.

"Give me that!" I ordered.

Juliet reluctantly handed her muffin over. I stuck it under my nose and inhaled. There was no mistaking the intense, eggy smell. It was even stronger than it had been in the juice.

"Purple carrots!"

I had been right about muffins—adults can hide stuff in them. I had also forgotten there was such a thing as carrot cake—the worst of the cakes—and these were carrot cake muffins. Concentrated carrot cake muffins, judging from the smell. Mayor Lapin was stuffing the locals full of more carrots.

"Don't eat the muffins!" I yelled out to the crowd. "Put down your muffins! Nobody should—"

Juliet screamed.

My warning had come ten seconds too late.

CHAPTER SEVENTEEN
THE TAN MAN'S PLAN

Everyone around us began to squeak and burp and gag like a bunch of guppies choking on bait. A large woman with long, red hair shrank to the size of an abnormal bunny right in front of me.

With a hiss and a whiz and a pop of goo she disappeared into her clothes.

One by one, people popped and shook. Some knocked over tables and chairs as they struggled. Some just seemed to disappear. The entire crowd was transforming into piles of clothes with fat, furry, cute bunnies wiggling out from under them. I clung to my uncle with my left arm and held onto Juliet's furry arm with my right.

"What's happening?" Rain cried.

"It's the muffins!" I hollered. "There must be a megadose of carrot juice in them. It's changing everyone rapidly!"

Rain threw his muffin across the food court like it had cooties. As soon as it landed, bunnies hopped over to it and started devouring the disgusting wad of cake.

The crowd was alive with the sound of chairs clanking against the floor and high-pitched wailing.

Everyone except Juliet, Rain, and I were now full-on mutant bunnies of every imaginable color. Fluffy fur was flying everywhere. It looked like the food court was a stuffed-animal farm that had just exploded on top of a pile of clothing.

Towering over all the fully transformed bunnies, Juliet and Rain and I stood out like sore and confused thumbs. I saw Mayor Lapin standing on the edge of the fountain, still holding the microphone and gazing at the strange crowd. I couldn't believe that he had done this intentionally to his own community. My tentacles wilted and my three squid hearts broke.

"Perfect," the mayor said into the microphone, addressing his staff. "Everything seems to be working out according to plan."

One of the staff pointed at us and yelled, "What about them, boss?"

With my furry uncle in my arms and Juliet and Rain

on both sides of me, I tried to look braver than I felt. I thought of Admiral Uli and Stacy Horse in "Mystery of the Withered Coral." The two of them had gone up against a group of shady aquarium owners, and Admiral Uli only defeated them because he had multiple tentacles and a barnacle bomb. I only had a long-eared bunny uncle and two slowly mutating friends.

"Perry Owens," Mayor Lapin said into his microphone, staring at me with his dark eyes. "How is it that you are still you?"

"I hate vegetables," I yelled, loud enough so he could hear.

"Well, no matter," the mayor said. "You are a child, and in the history of all time, I don't believe a child ever stopped a genius from doing what they needed to do."

"Should we run for it?" Juliet asked as we kept our eyes on the smiling mayor.

"I don't understand," Rain said. "I thought mayors were supposed to be good."

"Not all of them," I said in a hushed voice. "Once Admiral Uli was almost killed by Mayor Mollusk over a crooked clam deal."

Both of them stared at me.

"He was the mayor of Coral City," I explained.

"Please focus, Perry," Juliet said softly. "We need a plan."

"I've got this," I whispered. "Don't worry. I've read a ton of comic books."

Juliet looked worried.

"So, children," the Mayor said into the microphone. "Why don't you just come here and have a delicious muffin?"

"Okay," I said. "But Juliet still doesn't believe you planned all of this. She doesn't think you're smart enough."

If comics had taught me anything, it was that evil geniuses loved to give extended monologues about how brilliant their plans were. You just needed to get them talking.

Mayor Lapin's eyes lit up.

"Not smart enough?" He held the microphone up to his dry lips. "Let me tell you about smart. You see, I want to bring Bunny Island into a new and better era. The locals want this place to be a free-spirited and run-down haven for lazybones and dirtbags. I want to build something remarkable: a lucrative tourist destination that no admirer of cuteness could possibly resist. Is that too much to ask? I think not. I have tried and tried to be fair, but they're so stubborn. I gave them the opportunity to sell their homes and leave, but they refused. Nobody wanted change, so I made them change. That's when I formed the Bunny Island Remodeling Project, or BIRP."

The dumb, red T-shirts now made sense—they were

still dumb, but they made sense.

I looked around at the staff and at all the large adorable mutant bunnies on the ground. The rabbits were hopping over each other and nibbling on muffin crumbs. Some were sitting on the tables and a few were perched on chairs. None of them was paying attention to what was happening.

"These adorable rabbits will be kept in here until they sign over their land and houses," the mayor blathered on. "Then, I will sell the land to a developer who has been waiting to do business with me. The island will be remodeled. Some of the less-than-desirable things will have to go. Once things are remodeled, Bunny Island will become the most sought-after vacation destination in the world!"

Mayor Lapin laughed a wicked laugh, which caused him to cough violently. One of his burly staff members had to slap him on the back until he stopped choking. It was not very impressive.

"Anyhow," he finally continued. "There is one last detail. I'm sorry to say that it's rather unsanitary to have *quite* so many real bunnies here. We'll have to thin the herd a bit."

"You can't do that," Juliet yelled.

"Oh, I'm afraid you are mistaken, Juliet. I'm already doing it. Of course, I won't harm any of these good mutated bunnies here. No, I promise that if they sign over things to me, I will turn them all back into their old selves. A simple signature, and then they're welcome to the antidote."

Mayor Lapin pulled a small, clear plastic bag from out of his sports coat. It was filled with something brown and yellow.

"What is it?" I asked him.

"Oh, wouldn't you like to know. This is one of my best-kept secrets."

Mayor Lapin opened the bag and stuck his nose in it. He breathed in deeply.

I looked around for ideas, but the mall was filled with useless stores that sold things like clothing and vitamins. I tried desperately to remember one single comic where Admiral Uli was trapped in a mall and had to steal an antidote from a mayor. I couldn't. It was now all up to us.

"I can help," Rain whispered. "Let me distract the mayor while you grab the antidote. I owe you for some of the things I've done."

"That's true," I whispered.

"What are you kids whispering about?" the mayor asked into the microphone. "It's very rude. I've had the decency to address the whole group."

I looked at Rain—he was at least one-quarter rabbit, but he was 100 percent determined to help.

"Okay," I said. "You rush the mayor, and I'll try to get the antidote. Then we all make a break for any door that's not guarded."

"Again," Mayor Lapin said. "Whispering is very unattractive and a really poor social behavior. I would think that after hearing a powerful plan like mine you would—"

Without warning Rain lunged forward screaming, "Bunzai!"

With Zeke under my arm and Juliet by my side, I ran around some tipped-over tables and dodged some fat rabbits, straight toward the fountain. The mayor was so shocked by the sudden attack that he slipped on the edge of the fountain and fell backward into the water.

Zeke jumped out from under my arm and bit the mayor's hand, hard. The bag of antidote flew high into the air. Red-shirted goons raced in to help their leader, but not before Rain jumped into the fountain and tackled the mayor. I reached out and grabbed the antidote as it fell.

As Rain and the mayor thrashed around, water splashed up and soaked Juliet and me.

"Perry!" Juliet yelled. "Over there!"

I wiped my eyes and saw some staff members charging toward us.

I grabbed Juliet's hand, which, by the way, was really

soft and furry, and pulled her away from the crowd of mutant bunnies surrounding us. Everything was happening so fast that the staff didn't have time to react. We burst through a brown metal door at the far end of the food court before anyone could stop us.

"Run!" I ordered.

Behind the door was a long, dark service hall that was filled with pipes and air ducts. There were also a bunch of boxes stacked up high, all along the back wall. I spotted a large air-conditioning duct above the boxes.

"Come on!"

I scurried up the boxes and right into the opening at the end of the vent, Juliet right behind me. As soon as we had scrambled in deep enough that Mayor Lapin's cronies wouldn't find us, we stopped. We were both cramped in the vent, but we kept still and tried to control our breathing. It was almost impossible to calm my nerves. What made it worse was that Zeke and Rain still hadn't come through the doors.

"Where are they?" I whispered.

"The mayor had Zeke," Juliet panicked. "I think they got Rain, too."

I heard the metal door open, and two of the staff members stepped into the dark hallway. They looked around and checked some of the boxes, but they never looked up.

"They're not here," one said to the other.

"Who cares? They're kids. Besides, Erwin got the other two."

The men walked back out the door.

Juliet and I kept perfectly still inside the air duct.

"What do we do?" she asked. "I'm still turning into a mutant bunny, and they have your uncle and Rain. At least I still have my clothes but probably not for long. I'm sorry I didn't believe you, Perry. Me turning into a rabbit is way less believable than a talking squid or human-sized newts."

"Thanks," I said. "Admiral Uli would be impressed with everything you've been through and done so far."

I think Juliet smiled at that, but I couldn't tell for sure because it was pretty dark.

"This feels a little hopeless," she said after a moment.

"It's always darkest before the prawn," I said. "Besides, we have this." I pulled the bag of antidote from my pocket.

"You caught it?"

I nodded.

"Open it, quick!"

I tore open the small, clear bag. Instantly, I could tell what the antidote was. My nose had experienced that smell a thousand times.

"Crushed potato chips?" I said. "What the . . . ?" I took a pinch of the golden crumbs and held them up to my nose. They smelled like potato chips and looked like potato chips, but there was only one way to make sure. I put the pinch in my mouth and swirled it around.

"Well?" Juliet asked.

"They're potato chips," I said, disappointed.

We had been duped. There was no antidote. The mayor had tricked the bunnies into believing there was, just so they would sign the papers.

"I can't believe it," Juliet whispered. "What are we going to do now?"

"Well, I'm not going to waste these."

I took a handful of the fake antidote and began chewing. It tasted amazing, but it wasn't good enough to help me forget the trouble we were in.

Juliet reached her hand into the bag and took a pawful.

"It's delicious," she said as she cried and chewed.

"I'm sorry I got mad at you," I said, pouring the last bits of chips into my mouth.

"It's okay," she said, sniffling. "I shouldn't have said those things."

"It was my fault."

I don't know what it was, but something about listening to Juliet cry and being squeezed inside an air duct while my life was falling apart made me a little emotional.

"Do squids cry?" Juliet asked.

"They do now."

The two of us sniffed and choked back tears until I heard a strange hissing noise coming from Juliet's direction. I turned toward her, and even in the dark I could see what was happening. Her long ears were retracting, and her whiskers were gone. Her eyes were changing from huge to normal, while the hair on her arms and hands flew off and settled in the air duct. There was some popping and some clicking followed by a loud smacking noise. And in less than three seconds she was back to her old self. We both looked at each other with our jaws open and our eyes wide.

"It worked," she exclaimed. "It worked!"

"I can't believe it."

"The antidote is potato chips?"

"That's probably why the mayor's banned junk food," I said.

Juliet started to cry harder.

"What's the matter?"

"If the antidote's potato chips, then for Salty's sake, we're doomed. This island has nothing like that."

"Actually," I said. "That's not completely true."

Juliet perked up.

"What would you say if I told you that I not only know where some snacks are, but I also have a plan?"

"You do?" she asked.

I did, and there wasn't a moment to spare.

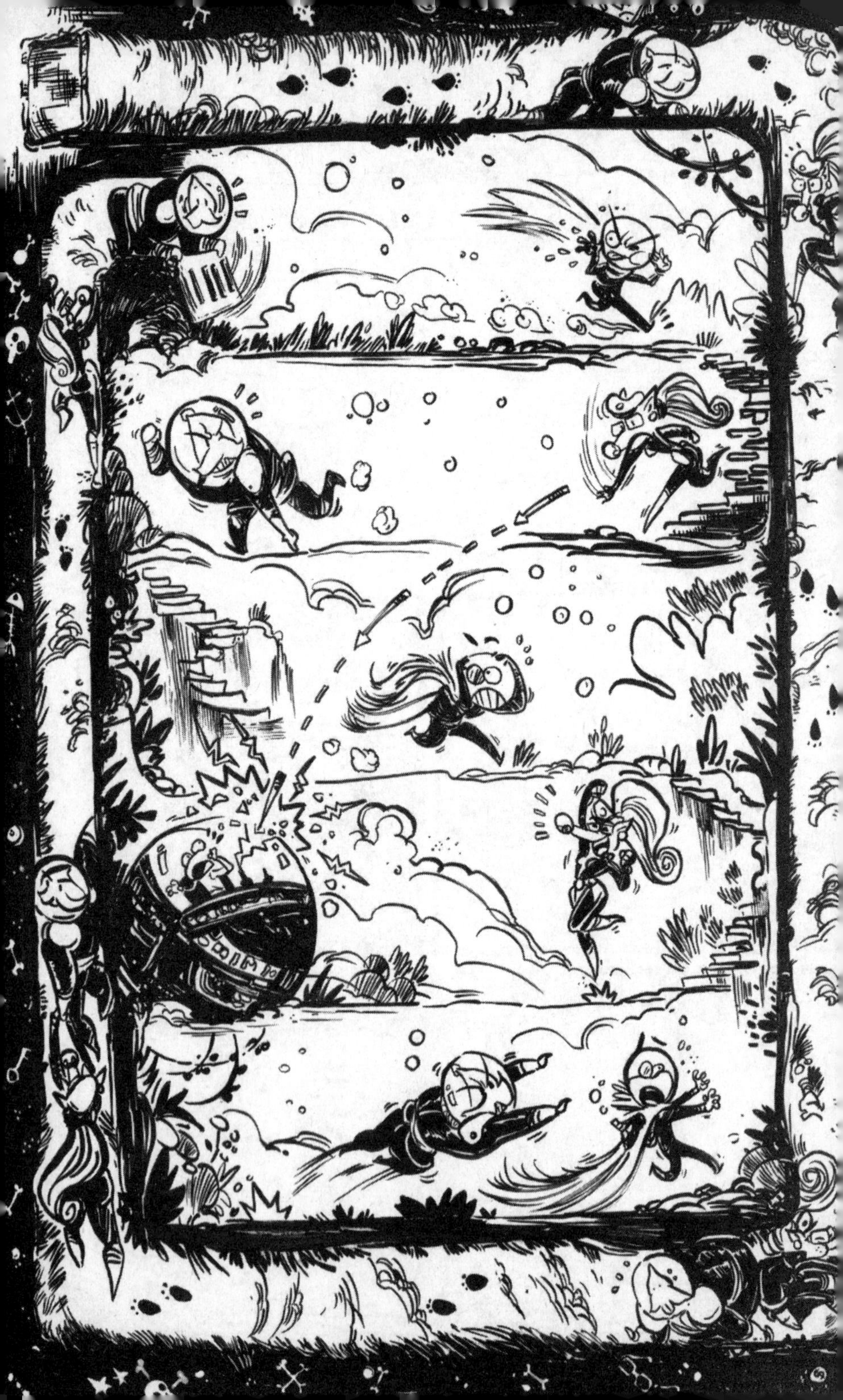

CHAPTER EIGHTEEN
A CRUMBLE RUMBLE

I quickly told Juliet my plan. It was pretty simple, but it would require the help of the mutant bunnies we'd left behind in the trees outside the mall. After I explained it, we climbed out of the air duct, and Juliet took off down the long storage hallway to find a way outside.

"Cod speed," I whispered.

Juliet would take care of her part. Now I just needed to get into position. On tiptoes, I slipped out of the storage area and back into the mall. Just before it inched shut, I propped the storage door open with a trash can to make sure I could escape to the hallway again quickly if I needed to. I kept myself low to the ground and scurried from storefront to storefront. I paused in the shadowy entrance of a store called Nuts about Fiber.

My three hearts were beating like crazy.

Hiding by the fiber store, I saw that all the tables and chairs in the food court had been pushed away from the fountain. The mutant bunnies were no longer hopping around and disorganized. They were all lined up in rows. The red-shirted staffers were holding long metal pinchers—the kind that I'd seen my dad use to get things off high shelves. A staffer reached out and snapped the pinchers at a nervous-looking bunny to keep it in line.

Quietly, I tiptoed over to the entrance of an exercise store called Fitness Bliss.

"This mall has the worst stores," I whispered to myself.

I moved behind a tall potted fern. From where I was, I could see everything perfectly. Mayor Lapin was at the front of the bunny lines with a couple of his men. Seeing him standing there, all tan and smiley, made me sick. But, as disgusted as I was, I was even more upset by what I saw to the side of him. Just to the left of the fountain was a cage containing both Zeke Bunny and Rain Bunny.

My ink boiled!

Mayor Lapin began to address the neat lines of hostage bunnies.

"Listen up," he ordered. "We have all the necessary paperwork here. I know it's not easy for a bunny to hold a pen, so we will assist you. I don't want any excuses. You are simply mutated humans; you still know how to sign your names. So, sign away your land and your homes, and your lives can return to normal."

I knew I needed to buy some time so that Juliet could get back. I didn't think she'd make it before any of the locals gave up their homes.

"Get them signing," the mayor commanded his men. "I want these deals locked up now."

The rabbits shook and squeaked in distress. The staff members cooed and said, "Aww."

"Knock it off!" the mayor yelled. "Don't look at them."

Two men tried to make the first bunnies in line sign the papers, but the rabbits refused.

"They're not doing it, mayor."

"Do I have to do everything myself?" Mayor Lapin stormed over to Uncle Zeke's cage and opened it up. He pulled my uncle out and held him, dangling by his back legs. My uncle squeaked twice, and the staff members had to look away for fear of being overwhelmed by cuteness.

"Okay, bunny-people. See this rabbit?" the mayor seethed. "Well, if you don't do as I say, I will take you one by one and hold you in the water until you are no longer as cute. Or breathing."

A large orange rabbit at the front of the line started to sign.

"Actually," the mayor said, "maybe I'll just drown this rabbit anyway."

Mayor Lapin held my uncle over the fountain and began to lower his adorable head toward the water.

"Hurry up, Juliet," I whispered, beginning to sweat.

The mayor lowered Zeke even farther.

I reached into my pocket and slipped on my mask.

Zeke was getting close to the water now.

I couldn't wait a second longer. I jumped from behind the fern and walked directly toward the crowd.

"Stop!" I shouted. I held one hand straight up in the air, imagining tentacles waving powerfully around me.

All heads, eyes, and ears turned toward me. For a second it was quiet. Even the rabbits paid attention.

"Stop what you're doing!" I said again, loudly.

The mayor smiled, his one crooked tooth peeking out from his lips.

"Perry? You just can't stay away. Such a harmless fool."

Cephalopods hate to be called harmless.

"Let go of my uncle!" I ordered.

"Oh," the mayor smiled. "This is Zeke. Perfect. I never liked Zeke."

He continued to lower him until Zeke's nose grazed the surface of the water.

"Wait!" I yelled. "What if I give myself up, and you let him go instead?"

"You're hardly in a position to make deals. But I'm feeling kindhearted. I might let your uncle go if you take a sip of some superconcentrated carrot juice and become a bunny, too."

"You mean you want me to drink some juice?" I asked nervously.

"Yes. Become a rabbit and your uncle lives."

I gazed at my uncle as he dangled.

"How about this," I reasoned. "No juice, but you can tie me up?"

"No deal," the mayor said.

"Okay, what if I do a juice fast? I promise not to drink any juice for the rest of my life, and then you don't hurt them."

The mayor reached into his sports coat and pulled out a small vial of something that was so purple it was almost black.

I gulped and began to feel faint.

"This is superconcentrated Purple Pow carrot juice. One taste and you've saved your uncle. Say no, and he takes a deadly swim."

I looked at Rain in the cage. I don't mean to be rude, but would it have killed him to break out of his cage right then and stop the mayor from making me take a drink?

"Time's ticking," the mayor said impatiently. "It's now or never."

"And you promise that if I drink it you won't hurt him?" I said, still trying to buy some more time for Juliet to arrive.

"I promise," Mayor Lapin said.

I walked slowly toward the fountain.

I could feel the crowd holding their collective cute breath and watching my every move. I stopped a couple of feet from the mayor, and he reached out and offered me the juice.

I knew there was an antidote on the way, but I still wasn't thrilled about drinking concentrated carrot juice or becoming a rabbit.

"Take a drink."

I lifted the bottle toward my mouth slowly. The smell of egg filled my nostrils, and my throat began to constrict. I felt nauseous, but I had no other choice.

"Tell me again about your plan?" I tried.

"Stop stalling," he ordered. "Drink!"

"Hold your sea horses."

I put the bottle to my lips and took a swig. My eyes went wide, and the hair on the back of my neck and tentacles stood up. Rain was right—it tasted like supercheesy pizza, nachos, and doughnuts mixed together. Maybe I had vegetables all wrong.

I quickly took another drink.

"Wow," Mayor Lapin said, bothered. "Don't drink so

much. That stuff is strong. Two drops can instantly . . ."

My head grew light, and my vision went gray. I felt my body rocking back and forth, and then, like an elevator dropping, I fell straight to the floor. I shook my head and felt my long ears swinging back and forth. My nose twitched, and my teeth grew while making a sort of creaking noise. My arms and legs shook like the static on an old TV.

Pop!

I stumbled out of my clothes and onto the ground. Looking left I saw a paw—my paw! There was no doubt about it—I was bunnified.

My arms tingled and my legs thumped. I looked around, but it was difficult to see very well because my mask was still wrapped around my head.

Glancing up, I could see Mayor Lapin. He was reaching down toward me! I shook the mask from my head to see better, but it came off a little too late. The mayor grabbed my furry torso and picked me up. He lifted me in front of his face, so close I could have touched his long, crooked tooth, and looked directly into my eyes.

"I must admit, Perry, you are much more appealing in rabbit form."

I twitched my nose and wriggled my whiskers.

"I also must admit that I don't feel like keeping my word today. Let's finish you off. Maybe I'll make a nice furry hat out of you and a pair of gloves out of your uncle."

This was not the way I thought I would die. I always thought I would go out in a blaze of glory, fighting crime in the Galapagos Galaxy with Admiral Uli. Instead, I was going to become some sort of fuzzy hat. My life flashed before my eyes. Thanks to my time on Bunny Island, it was finally starting to look like the adventures I'd always read about. Things were just getting good for me. I couldn't let it end now.

As the mayor held me up, I twisted my head to the left and sunk my teeth into his tan hand.

I bit down like a shark chomping on eel jerky.

Mayor Lapin's dark eyes bulged, and he screamed in pain, dropping me. I felt the wind rush out of my lungs as I hit the floor. I stood on my hind legs and tried to shake off the dizziness clouding my brain.

Looking over my shoulder, I saw the mayor still clutching his injured hand and yelling. After shouting a few words that no squid cadet would ever repeat, he screamed,

"Get that rabbit!"

Being so low to the ground, it was hard for me to see clearly. I noticed flashes of red T-shirts to my left and right, and I knew that his staffers were near. I scrambled over piles of clothes as one of the red shirts dove for me and missed by an inch. I knew where I needed to go. I only hoped Juliet had things in place.

I scrambled to the right, zigged left, and then full-on sprint-hopped as fast as I could toward the propped-open metal door. I scampered through it and up onto the boxes. I could hear at least two men behind me.

I hopped into the air duct.

The men reached into the vent. I pawed and jumped my way up a slanted section of the vent that took me even higher.

One of the big men had squeezed through the opening and was trying to pull himself in to get at me.

"Stay there, you dumb bunny!" he hissed.

I scrambled higher.

I moved up into a larger air duct that ran horizontally. After a few hops, the metal tunnel opened into a cavernous space above the ceiling of the food court. Air ducts ran in all directions, and I was now sitting on a vent directly above the angel bunny fountain.

The light coming through the slats of the vent cover allowed me to see my reflection on the glossy side of the air duct. I blinked my big blue eyes and tossed my long brown fur. I hate to say it, but I was adorable. If all of this went wrong and I had to spend the rest of my life as a rabbit, I'd probably have a ton of admirers.

Peering down through the slats, I could see the whole food court. Mayor Lapin had wrapped the hand that

I had bitten and was forcing pens into all the mutant bunnies' paws.

"You will sign, or you will be sorry," he shouted.

We had failed. I was worried about Juliet, but I was just as worried about my uncle and Rain and Flower and the other Bunny Islanders that were now being forced to give up everything they had.

I couldn't think of anything else to try or any comic that might help me. Admiral Uli had never been turned into a handsome rabbit before. The closest he had ever been to my situation was when Figgy Newton had turned his water heater's dial up to boiling, so that when Uli went to take a bath the water was way too hot. Sure, all he had to do was turn off the faucet, but for a moment he had been in hot water.

Now I was in some hot water of my own.

Just then, something to my right squeaked at me. When I turned to see what it was, I saw all the lost bunnies sitting in the vent and looking at me. Each one had a bag of chips in its mouth—all my favorite brands. Juliet had come through beautifully.

I raised my right paw and said, "Weerrt, weeert, berp berp?"

Even I didn't understand the bunny gibberish I was saying. I think I was attempting to say, "What are you waiting for? Let's do this."

"Weerrt, weeert, berp berp?" I tried again.

I hopped up, squealing and waving at the others, and pointed toward the big central vent on which I was standing. Like an army of well-trained stuffed animals, the bunnies all began moving toward the vent and tearing at their chip bags.

I turned to the lost bunnies and yelled, "Errrreeet!"

We all pounded our legs and kicked up a cloud of pure salt, additives, oil, and sugar. The cloud dropped through the vent like junk food rain. Some lost bunnies, stationed by other air vents, released their own bags of chips, and in a few seconds the entire food court looked like it was in the middle of a salty sandstorm. The rabbits below wasted no time munching at the air and getting a taste of the antidote. The falling chips filled the fountain, and immediately, there were splashes of yellow chip water flying everywhere.

"What's happening?!" I heard the mayor yelling from beneath me.

I kept stomping.

The pounding of paws on chips was so loud, I considered trying to plug my ears. But I didn't want to miss a second of what was happening below. The food court was alive with the noise of popping and hissing, as every mutant bunny began to change back into their human forms. There was also an excessive amount of belching and gasping and slipping and falling. On top of the wet antidote, there seemed to be a thick layer of gross goo coating the floor in the areas where bunnies were turning into people.

"Stop this!" the mayor screamed.

As he screeched, more and more bunnies returned to their former selves. People began yelling and hollering at him. Some smart-thinking folks grabbed a bunch of towels from a store called Bubba's Big Towels and threw them into the crowd. Mayor Lapin took one look at the angry gathering, flipped his slicked-back hair, and cried, "Retreat!"

The entire Bunny Island Remodeling Project committee slipped and stumbled as they fought to run away. After some awkward falls and a few hits and kicks from the crowd, they took off, splashing through the yellow chip water with towel-clad locals chasing after them.

The food court exploded with shouts of happiness and relief as the final stragglers returned to their previous shapes. Through the vent, everything looked like a yellow mess or the aftermath of a newt-nado. It was probably good that everyone was covered in wet chip pulp and big towels because everybunny—I mean everybody—still needed to find their clothes.

I stopped crushing chips and raced back through the

air ducts and climbed down the boxes. I then joined the crowd near the fountain and happily lapped up bits of chips that had mixed with the water and created a pool of antidote.

It was the tastiest transformation of my life.

CHAPTER NINETEEN
UNCLE

I stumbled out of the mall looking like a mess but feeling like a million clams. In a rush to cover ourselves, all of us former bunnies had grabbed whatever clothing we could find. So we were dressed in ill-fitting and embarrassing outfits. I had on a purple shirt and some big pants. All of us were coated in wet potato chip crumbs. My heart hurt at the loss of so many good chips, but the sacrifice seemed well worth it. Mayor Erwin Lapin had been served justice, salty squid–style.

I don't want to be mean, but while it was great to see everyone as humans again, the locals weren't quite as adorable as they had been in bunny form.

I couldn't find Juliet or Rain, but as I pushed past a

group of locals who were standing there, marveling over how trippy their day had been, I ran into a man rushing back toward the mall. We bumped shoulders, and when I turned to look at him I gasped.

"Uncle Zeke?"

He stepped back and looked at me with surprise.

"Perry!"

We both stood there with wide eyes and open mouths. He was covered in chip dust and wrapped in a *Finding Nemo* beach towel, which I remembered was an almost-identical outfit to the one he had worn when he last came to Ohio and took me swimming. Yes, his hair was a mess and his mustache was crumb filled, but his eyes were as happy and alive as they had always been. I didn't know what to do, so I stuck out my hands and made a *V* with my two main fingers on each one.

My uncle did the same.

I crossed my arms at the wrist and our fingers connected so we could link pinkies and swing our arms from side to side: the Uli salute of pride and victory.

We dropped our hands, and he gave me a hug similar to the one Admiral Uli had given Figgy after the Great Barrier Reef robbery. Of course, Admiral Uli was trying to squeeze the life out of Figgy, and my uncle was making me glad to be alive instead. People walked around us, talking excitedly and cheering about being human again.

I pretended that they were cheering for me and my uncle.

The hug ended, and Zeke stepped back to look at me, his hand still on my shoulder.

"You did it," he said.

"We made a promise," I reminded him.

"I'm a lucky uncle."

"Perry!"

I heard Juliet call my name and turned around to find her. Before I could say anything, she had her arms around me and was hugging me like Zeke had. "Perry, your plan worked!"

She had run to my uncle's house, gotten my suitcase, and brought the chips to the lost bunnies—who had done just what she asked them to do. My plan had worked. But I have to admit that even though the celebratory hug wasn't part of the plan, it was my favorite bit.

"Thank you, Juliet," I said, embarrassed. "I couldn't have done it without you."

"You're welcome, Perry."

She let go of me to fuss over Zeke and told us that she had seen Rain, who was back to his old self, helping people who were still in the mall.

"You guys did an amazing thing." Zeke grinned.

"How did this even happen?" I asked. "I thought it was newts."

"It definitely seems like a plot Figgy would hatch,

but it was Erwin. A short while back, I received some mysterious seeds in the mail. I planted them, and they grew really fast. As I was pulling the first one from the ground, Mayor Lapin showed up in my backyard, asking to help. The mayor said he was familiar with that type of carrot, and he went into the kitchen, where he made a special recipe for carrot pie. It was so good that I ate the whole thing. The next thing I knew, I was a rabbit.

"Erwin ransacked my house looking for any seeds I hadn't used and then left. That's when I saw the orange envelope on the floor. I had already put your package together—I just hadn't sealed it. So I scratched out some cards as best I could and nudged them into the envelope. Then I licked the flap and sealed it with a few dozen thumps from my back foot. I pushed the package out the door and over to the mailbox. I got it to lean up against the post, hoping the mail carrier would see it. I guess he did."

"Wow," I exclaimed.

"I know, we have good mail carriers here," Zeke said proudly.

"I meant, wow about the whole story," I clarified.

"Right," Zeke said. "After that, my best guess is that Lapin started feeding the carrots to certain people on the island to test out the quickest way to make them transform. That's why the lost bunnies were changed first. Then when Flower began using the carrots in the juice that the locals loved, he made his move. He must have discovered that superconcentrated juice can mutate people instantly. He put the superconcentrate into those muffins, and POW, the locals that were slowly changing were transformed instantly, so he could put his plan into action all the more quickly."

"And the slime on the back porch and other places?" I asked. "What was that?"

"You might have noticed that when you make the final transformation, there's a popping noise. Not only do you turn into a rabbit, but it generates a lot of goo."

"That's not so sweet," Juliet said.

"I have an idea," Zeke said. "This place is going to be a mess for a while. How about we get out of here and clean ourselves up. Then we can go do something really fun. It's not every day that you're here on my island, and I think what you three pulled off calls for a celebration. We could take a boat out onto the ocean with Flower and Rain."

"I'm not drinking any smoothies," I said.

"Of course not. We'll bring the other snacks you brought and gorge ourselves on things that are bad for us."

Juliet and I both agreed to my uncle's plan as quickly and as loudly as we could.

CHAPTER TWENTY

FROM STINKY TO INKY

Amazingly, life returned to normal on Bunny Island. All the people who had once been somebunny were now their former selves. The rest of the Purple Pow carrots and concentrate were collected and put away someplace safe. Zeke wouldn't tell me where that safe place was. The only clue he gave me was that I would "dig the hiding space."

So I'm pretty certain the carrots were buried somewhere.

All the locals were happy about me helping to make things right. And the Bunny Mooners were also happy with me because with the mayor out, Bunny Island was still a really health-foodie place, but now there were more things to eat. Things that actually tasted good. Flower added a chocolate chip smoothie to her menu. One vending machine even had caramel-covered cookie dough balls in it.

Well, it did until I got to it.

Mayor Erwin Lapin and his staff were arrested and held in Bunny Island's tiny jail until they could be moved off the island and prosecuted in Florida.

Now, however, my stay on Bunny Island had come to an end. It had been a squidtastic couple of weeks, but it was time to return home to Ohio. Juliet and Rain came over to help me pack.

"This is a lot different from how I packed to come here," I told them as I gathered things to put into my suitcase.

My snacks were long gone, and this time I was filling my bags with things that really mattered. I wrapped up the seashells my uncle and I had found on the beach while searching the sand for newt-tail tracks. I packed the cool blue rock I had found in the clearing when all of us had gone there for a celebratory squid-fest. I put in the piece of driftwood that was shaped like an ink blaster. I had discovered it on the other side of the island, when we were hiking through the jungle and searching for newt nests.

"Here," Rain said. "Don't forget this."

Rain handed me my own Rain Train tank top. It was green and exactly like the ones he wore all the time.

"It's to remind you of your first day here."

"I'm glad I survived that."

I put the shirt into my suitcase, along with some shorts my uncle had bought me, and a couple of souvenirs I had bought for my dad.

"And this is from me," Juliet said.

She handed me her headphones.

"But these are yours."

"I know, but maybe you can put them on when you're in Ohio and think of us. Besides, I owe you."

"I'll wear them all the time."

I put the headphones around my neck and plugged the loose end into one of my pockets.

"Thanks, you guys. I don't think I'll ever forget you."

"I'm pretty memorable," Rain admitted.

"I think Admiral Uli put it best in *Ocean Blasterzoids* Issue #35 when he had to go to the town of Dorsal to catch the Mahi-Mob. He said, 'Today might be sad, but tomorrow is always salty.'"

Juliet and Rain nodded like they understood. Uncle Zeke came into the house smiling and holding something behind his back.

"Are you ready?"

I nodded and zipped up my suitcases.

"Wait," he said. "One last thing." From behind his back, he pulled out a rolled-up shirt. "I was afraid it wouldn't get here in time, but like I told you, we have really good mail carriers."

He handed me the shirt, and I carefully unrolled it. On the front were Admiral Uli, Stacy Horse, Commander Cod, and even Benedict Cucumber, who looked shifty.

"I got it on eBay. I just wish they had one in my size."

"Zeke! Thank you so much!"

I wanted to rip off the Admiral Uli shirt I was wearing and put on the new one, but I didn't feel like changing in front of company. So I tucked the shirt into my suitcase and zipped it up again.

"Should we go?" Zeke asked.

I looked at all three of them and wished I didn't have to.

CHAPTER TWENTY-ONE

AWKWARD

Being home was great, but I missed Bunny Island. I also missed my uncle and Juliet. Actually, I even missed Rain. He had called me yesterday from the glass phone booth to tell me that he saw a dead squid on the beach and thought of me.

I was horrified at my fallen comrade and touched that Rain would call me.

I was still spending a good amount of time in my room playing on the computer and reading comic books. But to be honest there were moments when I wanted to be running down Rabbit Road or stomping across the beach. My legs were actually mad about all the lying around I was now doing.

"Fine, legs," I said. "I'll stand up."

I closed the comic book I had just finished reading for the third time.

It was late morning, and my bedroom window was open so the breeze could come through. I wasn't worried about newts attacking, because they knew perfectly well that it would be foolish of them to mess with me.

Outside, my old friend Ryan pulled up to my house. I jumped at the chance to run to the front door.

"Hi, Ryan," I said when I opened the door.

"Please, kid, I'm not your friend."

"Right," I said sadly. "I guess you heard about Juliet and Rain, then."

Ryan "acted" like he didn't know what I was talking about.

"Just take this, please," he begged.

Ryan was holding what looked to be another orange envelope from Zeke containing the next issue of *Ocean Blasterzoids*.

"Sure," I agreed. "We shouldn't make this any more awkward than it needs to be."

Ryan handed me two envelopes.

"Two?" I asked in surprise.

He was already down the walk and driving off. I closed the door, looking closely at the envelopes.

My dad came out of the kitchen, where he had been grinding wheat into flour all morning.

"Anything for me?" he asked.

I put the orange envelope from Zeke under my arm and checked the second one. It was a small yellow one from Juliet.

"Nope," I said, blushing.

"Look at you," my father said proudly. "Getting a letter from someone you're not related to. It's like you came back from that island a player."

"What's a player?" I asked.

"I have no idea," my dad admitted.

We both stood there a moment as he cleared his throat and I finished blushing.

"Well," he finally said. "I was reading in the almanac that we can expect this to be a favorable summer for drought-tolerant crops. That includes certain kinds of wheat."

"I can't speak for wheat, but I know it's been a good one for me." Summer wasn't even halfway over, and already my head was filled with things I will never forget. I held up the orange envelope. "I'm going to read this new issue."

"Of course," my dad said. "It's really nice to have you home, squid."

"What'd you say?" I asked.

"Just that I'm glad you're back, kid," he said with a smile.

I returned the smile and ran outside to read.

ABOUT THE AUTHOR

Obert Skye is the author of the bestselling Leven Thumps series, the Creature from My Closet series, and the Witherwood Reform School series. As far as he knows, he has never been attacked by either bunnies or newts. There is still time, however. He lives in Arizona with his family. Learn more about him at www.obertskye.com.

ABOUT THE ARTIST

Eduardo Vieira is an illustrator who specializes in character design. He lives and works in Brazil. You can see more of his work at www.eduardovieirart.bigcartel.com.

YOU MAY ALSO LIKE THE HAMSTERSAURUS REX SERIES!

Beware: Rampaging mutant dino-hamster!

HARPER
An Imprint of HarperCollinsPublishers

www.harpercollinschildrens.com